SOMETHING WICKED

By. E. X. Ferrars

SOMETHING WICKED

E. X. FERRARS

PUBLISHED FOR THE CRIME CLUB BY
DOUBLEDAY & COMPANY, INC.
GARDEN CITY, NEW YORK
1984

M ✓

All of the characters in this book are fictitious,
and any resemblance to actual persons,
living or dead,
is purely coincidental.

Library of Congress Cataloging in Publication Data

Ferrars, E. X.
Something Wicked.
(Crime Club)
I. Title.
PR6003.R458S7   1984   823'.912
ISBN 0-385-19254-1

SOMETHING WICKED

CHAPTER 1

"But of course you must let me pay rent for the place," Professor Basnett said. "I couldn't think of staying there otherwise."

"No, really," Peter Dilly, his nephew, answered. "I don't want any rent. It's an advantage to me to have someone living there through the winter, seeing the pipes don't freeze and that squatters don't move in and settle, or burglars break in and steal my priceless treasures. If you'd really like to stay there, Andrew, you'll be more than welcome."

Though he was the son of Andrew Basnett's sister, who had died when Peter was a child, he had never called Andrew uncle in his life. As a child of three Peter had settled for Andrew and had stuck to it ever since. Peter was now thirty-five and Andrew was seventy.

"Of course I realize the money doesn't mean anything to you now," Andrew said, "but perhaps if I paid in cash so that the taxman needn't know . . ."

"That isn't the point," Peter said. "Don't you understand, I *like* the thought of you living there if it's got any attractions for you? I'm glad for once to be able to do something for you, instead of its always being the other way round. And a pretty small thing it is, as I've just explained, since I'd far sooner have someone living there for the next few months than just leave the place empty."

"Very well, if you're quite sure. I'm very grateful."

They were having lunch together in Soho. The attraction for Andrew Basnett of borrowing his nephew's cottage in the Berkshire village of Godlingham was that his own flat in St. John's Wood was about to be redecorated. At last, after seeing it grow shabbier and shabbier since the death of Nell, his wife, ten years ago, he had made up his mind to have it painted right through, had given a good deal of thought to the choosing of new colours, had felt interested and stimulated at the idea of change, and then had thought with horror of having to live in the midst of the upheaval while the work was in progress.

The men on the job would probably bring a radio with them, which they would play all day at its loudest. At intervals they would want cups of tea. They would discuss football at the tops of their voices. The quiet life, which was the only kind of life that Andrew could endure nowadays, would be shattered. In a state of sheer panic he had almost made up his mind to cancel the whole project when his nephew, as they were drinking sherry before this lunch that they were having together, had asked if by any chance Andrew would care to borrow the cottage in Godlingham, as Peter himself intended to spend the winter in Paris.

"It's only three miles from Maddingleigh, which is less than an hour from Paddington," Peter said, "so you could get up to London quite easily and keep on with your work, and my precious Mrs. Nesbit would come in once a week to do the cleaning, just as she does for me, and I expect you'd find the neighbours friendly if you felt like company, though you can be as quiet as you like if you want. I know you like walking, and the downs are there, right at the back door, for when you feel like it." He finished his sherry and put his glass down. "Just a suggestion," he said. "Think about it. No need to make up your mind on the spot. I just thought perhaps you might enjoy a change."

It did not take Andrew a moment to make up his mind. But then there followed the inevitable argument about the rent, though this was little more than a formality, since Andrew knew that Peter would refuse to accept any payment, as Peter had known that Andrew would do his best to insist on a normal businesslike arrangement between them. Luckily for both of them, the money was of little importance to either. Andrew, since his retirement three years ago, had an adequate pension as well as some investments left to him by Nell, and could easily afford to pay a reasonable rent, while Peter, who had started life as a schoolmaster but had recently discovered a knack for writing science fiction, which had turned out surprisingly successful, and who might almost be called rich, certainly had no need for any additional income. For his self-respect, however, each felt that there should be at least a token argument, though Andrew had known from the beginning that he would give in, since after all it was the rational thing to do, Peter being so obviously pleased to be able to make a generous gesture.

The work that Andrew was doing, to which Peter had referred, was the writing of a life of Robert Hooke, the noted seventeenth-century natural philosopher and architect, celebrated for pioneering microscopical work in a variety of fields, and particularly renowned as the first microscopist to observe individual cells. Andrew, who had been a professor of botany in one of London University's many colleges, had always felt a particular interest in him and for the last two years had made a habit of going twice a week to work on his papers in the library of the Royal Society in Carlton House Terrace. The first year after his retirement he had spent on a slow journey round the world, lecturing in the United States, New Zealand, Australia and India, but he had started his book soon after arriving home and had been absorbed in it ever since.

Whether it would ever be finished was a matter of uncertainty. As he kept destroying almost as much of it as he added to it week by week, it never seemed to grow any longer. Nevertheless, the work was important to him and one of the attractions of Peter's offer was that although Godlingham was in the country, the journey to London was so short that it would be easy to keep up those bi-weekly visits to the Royal Society.

Apart from that, Andrew knew the cottage, knew that it was comfortable, well heated, convenient and quiet. He had spent several week-ends there with Peter while he had still been a schoolmaster, teaching in the nearby school known as Newsome's, named after the family who had once inhabited what was now only a small portion of the buildings. Peter had left his job soon after his books had begun to sell successfully, but had kept on the cottage. Andrew knew that nothing could suit him better.

"When shall I take over?" he asked once the matter of the rent had been disposed of. He was thinking of the men with their radio and their cups of tea and their football talk and was hoping that after a brief talk with their foreman to make sure that he understood what was to be done, he could arrange to avoid them altogether. The key to the flat could be handed over to the porter, who was an obliging and responsible man and could safely be left in charge. "When are you leaving?"

"Next Friday," Peter said, "but you needn't hurry to get down before that unless you want to. I can leave a key with my next-door neighbour, Jack Fidler, and you can pick it up from him. I can't remember if you ever met him when he came down to see me. He's a teacher of biology at Newsome's. He'll be interested to meet you. I'll give you his phone number and you can ring him up when you want to collect the key."

"I don't think I've met any of your neighbours," Andrew said, "except for a tall, diffident individual who came once to return a book. But seeing a stranger there, he vanished as fast as he could."

Peter smiled. "That sounds like Godfrey Goodchild." Peter's smile was bright and lit up his pale, deceptively blank face very charmingly. He was a small man and in a neat, small way was good-looking, with small, fine hands and fair, straight hair which he kept thrusting back from his forehead, but which instantly tumbled forward again almost into his grey eyes. "Godfrey's retired, I'm not sure from what. He doesn't talk about himself and makes you feel it would be the height of impertinence to question him. He's my next-door neighbour on the other side from the Fidlers. He and Hannah have been living there since long before I moved in and we're quite good friends, but it's extraordinary how little I know about him."

'Surprising, considering how curious you are about people," Andrew said. He was much taller than his nephew and in fact, if he took the trouble to stand erect, was even taller than he looked, but in the last few years he had allowed himself to get into the habit of stooping. He was a spare man with bony features, short grey hair and grey eyes very like Peter's, under eyebrows that were still black. His long sight was still good and he needed glasses only for reading. "You must do a lot of listening and watching when you look as if you're thinking about nothing at all."

Peter shook his head. "The people I write about are complete fictions. They couldn't possibly exist. I don't have to tell you that, do I? I don't think I'm at all clever at understanding real people. For instance, I've never been able to make up my mind about our murderess."

"Your *what?*"

"Our murderess. Do you remember the house on the hillside opposite mine—good Georgian, red brick, nice parapet round the roof, fine windows and a rather handsome portico.

It's called Godlingham House and our murderess lives there."

"I remember it, but I never met the lady. What kind of murders does she go in for?"

"Oh, there was only one, if that. That's what I've never been able to make up my mind about. Did she do it or didn't she?"

"You know her well?"

"Hardly at all, and you aren't likely to meet her. She keeps herself very much to herself."

"What was her sentence?"

"Oh, my goodness, she wasn't sentenced. She wasn't even charged. She had a perfect alibi."

"Then doesn't that answer your question? She didn't do it."

Peter made one of his attempts at thrusting back his hair. "Ye-es. One has to accept that. But one can't help wondering . . ."

"Who was it you think she may have murdered?" Andrew asked.

"Her husband."

"Why?"

"Oh, for money. He was immensely rich. He was a brother of Henry Hewison's—you know, the man who started Newsome's. The two brothers inherited a lot of money when they were in their forties or thereabouts from some rich relative, and Henry put all his money into the school, which has always been his passion, while Charles, the elder . . . But you don't want to know all this. As I said, you won't meet her."

"I'm very interested." If Peter had written detective stories instead of science fiction, Andrew would have read them eagerly. As it was, he had tried to read them out of affection for Peter, but had given them up. He admitted that Peter wrote very well and sometimes used his fantasies to make comments of some penetration on social affairs. His first book, called *Whalewater,* was about a species of whale that had learnt to fly and which mankind had naturally recognized at once as a most valuable addition to their stockpile of armaments, since these amiable and very teachable mammals, which had not the imagination to know fear, could be both airships and submarines. Peter's second book, *Camellords,* was about some scientists who by a remarkable feat of genetic engineering had managed to create men with the heads of camels. These, unfortunately, had had all the hauteur of the camel together with all the most aggressive instincts of man, and had soon established an élite that had gradually reduced ordinary men to helpless slaves, a condition which it turned out they enjoyed. It had been obvious to Andrew that Peter, whose subject had been classics, had no fragment of knowledge about genetic engineering, but then neither had his readers, and the book had sold very well and had had a television series based on it.

"Well then," Peter went on, "the rumour was that Charles Hewison was going to put a lot of money into his brother's school, which wasn't flourishing quite as was hoped and had eaten up most of H.H.'s capital. H.H. is what we always called Henry Hewison. Charles had been in the Foreign Service, living mostly abroad until he retired, when he bought Godlingham House and came to live there to be near his brother. Charles was married, Henry isn't. I believe Charles married fairly late in life a woman who was at least twenty years younger than he was and had a daughter. I remember when they first came to the place they were friendly, sociable sort of people and were generally liked and seemed to be happy enough with one another. And then one evening Charles Hewison was murdered."

"How long ago was that?" Andrew asked.

"About six years," Peter said. "It happened just after Christmas. There was a big freeze-up at the time—d'you remember it? It was fearsomely cold and as we had a power failure in the district at the time that cottage of mine was like an icebox. I hope nothing of the sort happens to you this year, because, as you know, I'm entirely dependent on electricity. There isn't a fireplace in the house. The central heating's oil-fired, but of course there's an electric pump and that wouldn't work, so the radiators went stone-cold. The cut lasted for about two days and snow had blocked the road to Maddingleigh and I'd been fool enough not to buy one of those portable gas heaters—you'll find there's one there now—and I couldn't get into Maddingleigh to buy one, so there was nothing for it but to sit there and freeze, though the neighbours with less modern, labour-saving houses than mine were very kind and brought me hot food and asked me in to sit by their fires."

"Just a moment," Andrew said, feeling that Peter was losing track of the subject in which he himself was interested. "How was Charles Hewison killed?"

"Shot through the head," Peter answered.

"What with?"

"Some gun or other. I don't know much about guns."

"Did it turn up afterwards?"

"No, it clean disappeared."

"What time of day did it happen?"

"Between five o'clock and five-fifteen."

"How can they be so exact?"

The first course of their lunch had just been delivered to them. Peter picked up his knife and fork and began on it.

"As I remember what I heard," he said, "Charles phoned H.H. at just about five o'clock. I believe it was something to do with Charles putting money into the school. Anyway, the police had H.H.'s word for it that Charles was alive at five. Then at about five-fifteen Mrs. Nesbit phoned Godlingham House and got no answer. She was working for the Hewisons as housekeeper at that time and she stayed on with Pauline

Hewison for a time after the murder, but then she got married and gave up the job. She just does a bit of daily work around the village these days. Well, it happened to be her day off and she'd gone to visit her sister in Maddingleigh and in the normal way would have come home in the evening. But the blizzard started sometime in the afternoon and the road back to Godlingham was blocked and the bus couldn't get through, so she tried telephoning the Hewisons to tell them she was stuck and wouldn't be home till next day. And she got no answer. So the police assumed that that was because Charles was dead already. Apparently that fitted quite well with what the pathologists had to say about it, and when the police came round the village and questioned us all about where we'd been and so on, that seemed to be the only time they were interested in."

"Where was Mrs. Hewison while all this was going on?" Andrew asked.

"Ah, that's the point," Peter said. "She was with the Fidlers, playing bridge—cutthroat, that's to say, because that evening there were only three of them, Jack and his wife Amabel and Pauline Hewison. The fourth person was normally H.H., but he'd rung up to say he couldn't get through the snow from Newsome's. He lives there in a flat at the top of the building. The place was empty, of course, except for him and the caretaker and one or two of the domestic staff, because the Christmas holidays were on."

"It was a regular arrangement for the four of them to play bridge, was it?"

"More or less, on Saturdays. Pauline Hewison sometimes went over to the Fidlers for tea about half past four and H.H. would turn up a bit later and leave in time to take the school prayers at eight o'clock."

"Charles Hewison was never in on it?"

"No, he didn't play bridge. He said it bored him."

"But when he was murdered Mrs. Hewison was definitely

with your friends, the Fidlers, playing cutthroat? You've their word for that?"

"Yes."

"Then I don't see where the problem about her arises. She couldn't have murdered her husband." Andrew looked thoughtfully at Peter's pleasant but unrevealing face. "Or don't you trust the Fidlers?"

Peter did not answer at once. Then, laying down his knife and fork, he said, "I told you, I'm not clever at understanding people. I like Jack, though he's got a vile temper. Sometimes I hear him shouting at Amabel in the garden in a way that makes me fear for her safety. Luckily it never seems to upset her. I've never seen her upset about anything. But the thing is, there's something about Pauline herself . . . I know this is highly slanderous, but she could so easily be a murderess."

Andrew laughed. "I'm glad you realize it's slanderous. Do you go around saying this sort of thing to many people?"

"I think this is the first time I've ever talked about it," Peter answered. "But a lot of other people still believe she did it. It's something in the woman herself that provokes it. And of course, she'd a whale of a motive. All that money that Charles was going to hand over to H.H."

"Suppose she did do it," Andrew said, "it means that the Fidlers lied on her behalf and that would be a pretty big risk for them to take. It would make them accessories after the fact. Are they very close friends, or perhaps even more than that? I was thinking, is there by any chance something between her and Fidler?"

"I'm sure there isn't," Peter said. "Jack and Amabel, after their fashion, which I admit wouldn't suit me if I ever got married, seem to be very happy together. I don't think Jack's ever cared for anyone else, and Pauline, even in the old days, never seemed to have more than a neighbourly, rather patronizing, bridge-playing sort of relationship with the Fidlers and nowadays doesn't have anything to do with them. She's cut herself off from everybody, lives alone in that great house except when her daughter visits her occasionally, and has a foreign couple to run the place for her, who change fairly frequently and don't mix much with the locals."

"Is that because she feels people think she's guilty?"

"It could be."

"Then why doesn't she simply move away? If she's got plenty of money, she could settle abroad or anywhere where people don't know the story."

"I know that's strange. I thought perhaps it might be pride."

"What about grief? Isn't that possible? Perhaps when she lost her husband she lost her interest in life. That can happen to a person." Andrew had believed it had happened to him when Nell died after her hopeless fight with cancer. Not many people had recognized how long the wound had taken to heal over, in so far as it ever had, and he had had work to help him. Not like the woman whom Peter had been describing, who lived alone in a big house with nothing to do and nothing to interest her, not even those evenings of bridge with her neighbours. "Was anyone ever charged with the murder?"

"No," Peter said. "I believe the police picked up a couple of boys who'd been in trouble before for break-ins and who'd been seen about the place, but there wasn't any real evidence against them and they were let go. But a window had been broken in the kitchen and someone had climbed in and some money had been taken, and there was no suggestion that the Hewisons had ever owned a gun, so the thing was written off as a robbery."

"And isn't that probably the truth?"

"I suppose so."

"I imagine with the snow there was no chance of finding footprints, or anything like that."

"No."

"Now about my going down to the cottage, Peter . . ."

Peter gave his cheerful smile again. "I hope my flow of gossip hasn't put you off the idea of going."

"Not at all. But I don't think I can get away before Friday. I'll have to arrange things with the decorators, if they're to do the job when I'm not there to keep an eye on them, and I'll have to get organized generally. I should think it'll be Tuesday or Wednesday next week before I can get down. So if you'll give me the telephone number of your friends who'll have the key, I'll get in touch with them when I know where I am."

Peter found an address book in a pocket, gave Andrew the Fidlers' number and Andrew wrote it down. They talked for a while then about Peter's plans for the winter, agreed, though at first Peter resisted the suggestion, that even if Andrew was to pay no rent he should at least pay Mrs. Nesbit's wages, and that he should have the use of Peter's car, which would be left in the garage. Andrew had no car of his own, holding that it was a waste of money to keep one in London, but he realized it would be an asset in the country. It was nearly three o'clock when, with affection on both sides and more thanks from Andrew, he and Peter parted, and Andrew, very pleased with the arrangements that had been made, made his way home to St. John's Wood by the underground.

In fact it was on Wednesday of the following week that he took the train down from Paddington to the small town of Maddingleigh and then took a taxi to the village of Godlingham. But on the Sunday before that he had telephoned the Fidlers to inquire when it would be convenient for him to pick up the key of Peter's cottage and the car-key. A deep, booming voice had answered him, announcing, "Fidler speaking."

"Mr. Fidler, my name is Basnett," Andrew said. "I believe my nephew, Peter Dilly, told you I shall be spending some time—"

"Ah yes, in the cottage," Jack Fidler interrupted. "And you want to pick up the keys. Splendid. I'm so glad you're coming, Professor. Much nicer than to have the place next door standing dark and empty all the winter."

"Thank you," Andrew said. "If you could tell me—"

"When to collect the keys. Any time you like. If I'm not here, Amabel's sure to be in."

"I'm planning to come down on Wednesday. I was thinking of taking the eleven-forty from Paddington, which gets down to Maddingleigh—"

"At twelve-nineteen," Andrew was told before he could say so himself. He had a feeling that Jack Fidler made a habit of interrupting people, using that fine voice of his to flatten out their less resonant tones. "Then you can take a taxi—there are always plenty at the station—and you'll get here in about a quarter of an hour. I'll almost certainly be at home, as I generally come home for lunch. Term hasn't broken up yet, there's still about a week to go, but the chances are I'll be here. And if not, as I said, Amabel will be in and can take you to the cottage and show you where everything is."

"It's very kind of you—"

"Not at all, not at all. We're looking forward to meeting you. And if there's anything we can lay in for you in advance —milk, I mean, bread, eggs, whisky, anything else you'd like, just let us know."

"It's very kind—"

"No trouble at all. There's an excellent shop in the village where you can get everything. Amabel will tell you all about it. Just make a list of what you want and let us have it before Wednesday and she'll see your refrigerator's stocked up for you. By the way, you are the Andrew Basnett who explored the development of metabolic activity in cells as they matured—"

"Yes, yes." It was Andrew's turn to interrupt. "We'll talk about it some other time. And again, thank you for your help. You're very kind."

He rang off swiftly, wondering uneasily if he would find Jack Fidler a little much to cope with. Andrew was a friendly man who in general enjoyed the company of many and varied people, but he had an illusion about himself that the one thing in life that he desired was peace and quiet. Actually he had a considerable fear of loneliness and at the back of his mind when he accepted Peter's offer there had been a faint dread that he might find himself too much alone in Godlingham and that for all its charm, he might soon find himself hankering for his London flat, decorators, radio, cups of tea and all. All the same, he did not like being interrupted and he did not want to find that his life was being organized for him by the firm hand of the obliging Amabel.

However, it was plain that the Fidlers had only meant to be friendly, and for a moment Andrew had thought that perhaps he really ought to make out the list of groceries that Jack Fidler had suggested so that he should not seem to be ungratefully rebuffing a well-meant offer. But then Andrew had reflected that as he would be arriving in Godlingham by lunch-time, he could eat in the village pub and then himself buy what he needed in that excellent shop that Fidler had mentioned. When Andrew set off for Paddington on the following Wednesday he had not been in touch with Fidler again.

The December day was very cold, the sky was a flat, dull grey, the trees to be seen from the train in their wintry bareness were dark and motionless. There had been frost in Maddingleigh and the puddles that had been left by recent rain in the car-park outside the station were slippery with

ice. Andrew skidded on one of them and nearly fell. He had
been athletic when he was young and still had not accustomed himself to the fact that at seventy it was wise to watch
with a certain caution where he was going when he strode
ahead.

He still walked fast, his long legs sticking to their old habit
of taking big strides, and it puzzled him a little that they
seemed to tire sooner than he thought they should. He had
brought two suitcases with him, one of them filled mostly
with books and papers and very heavy, but he had left his
typewriter behind, as Peter had assured him that there was
one in the cottage. Also, as Jack Fidler had said, there were
plenty of taxis waiting at the station.

Andrew hailed one, gave the driver the address of the
cottage in Godlingham and, looking at his watch as he settled back in his seat, saw that the train had been only ten
minutes late, which was not bad as things went nowadays.
Once he had picked up the keys and deposited his luggage
in Peter's cottage, he thought, he would go straight out to
the pub which he remembered having visited with Peter,
where they did a very good scampi and chips, then he would
unpack and get generally settled. It was pleasant to think
that the cottage would be warm, since the central heating
would have been left on for him by Peter, that the water
would be hot and that Mrs. Nesbit, whom Andrew had still
to meet, had promised to leave his bed made up for him. He
had a bottle of whisky in one of his suitcases and if he felt
inclined could spend a somnolent afternoon, allowing for
the trip that he must make to the shop to buy himself some
supper. Some more extensive shopping to cover his needs
for the next few days could be left till tomorrow.

Peter's cottage, which was beyond the Fidlers', over-
looked the main road from Maddingleigh to Reading, a little
before the turn-off into the village of Godlingham itself. The
two cottages were very similar in appearance, both of them

small, simple, white buildings, two storeys high, pleasant and unpretentious and only about fifteen years old. Each stood in a garden of about a quarter of an acre, set on a slope well above the road, so that the paths up to the front doors and the drive-ways to their garages were steep and today very slippery. The Fidlers' garden, bare as it was at this time of year of all but a few evergreen shrubs and a faint glimmering of frost on the dark soil of the empty flower-beds, looked noticeably better kept than Peter's. There were two other cottages, making a row of four on the slope there, one of them before the Fidlers' cottage and the other beyond Peter's. The first one of these was half-timbered and thatched and extremely small and had a certain air of neglect about it. The farther one was a square, red, early Victorian box with a slate roof and a great deal of ivy over its façade.

Facing these, on the upward slope on the other side of the road and set far back from it, was a handsome Georgian house that Andrew remembered, a building of great dignity with a background of fine woods. Except for a few pines and holly trees these were leafless now, but the twigs of beech and oak made a pleasing tracery against the leaden sky. Godlingham House, that was what Peter had told Andrew it was called.

He asked the driver to stop outside Peter's cottage, paid him, then was surprised and pleased, as it was not the sort of thing that happened often in London nowadays, when the man carried the two suitcases up the slippery slope to Peter's door. As the taxi drove off, Andrew returned down the path to the road, then climbed up the one next door to the Fidlers' house, rang the bell, almost immediately heard footsteps inside and the door was opened.

Jack Fidler was a younger man than Andrew had expected from the rich sound of his voice. He had expected someone of at least fifty with all the self-assurance of middle age. Instead he saw a man who was probably no older than Peter, although he was nearly bald already, with only a few strands of reddish hair plastered across the crown of his head. It made his forehead look very high and might have given an intellectual cast to his face if it had not been so round and plump, with slightly protuberant blue eyes, full, ruddy cheeks and a small, pouting mouth. He was of medium height and in spite of a noticeable paunch looked vigorous. He was wearing an old tweed jacket and corduroy trousers. He shot out a large, thick-fingered hand.

"Professor Basnett? So glad you got here safely. Nothing much in the way of a journey, of course. What about your luggage? Not left it in the road, have you?" The voice was the same that Andrew had heard on the telephone, though somehow, when it was not directed straight into his ear, it did not sound quite so powerful. "We're a pretty law-abiding neighbourhood on the whole, but you never know who's going to go by on the main road. We have our share of vagabonds and hooligans."

"As a matter of fact, I left it on Peter's porch," Andrew said. "I thought if you'd just very kindly give me the keys—"

"Yes, yes, the keys, of course," Jack Fidler said. "But you're coming in for a drink, aren't you? And Amabel's expecting you to lunch . . . No, no," he went on quickly as Andrew opened his mouth to speak, "no trouble at all. Nothing special, you know, just what we're having ourselves. You don't want to be bothered with getting something for yourself right away."

"It's very good of you," Andrew said, wondering how often he had already said this to Fidler, "but I ought to put my luggage indoors, and I thought I'd just go and have a snack at that pub in the village—"

"The Green Dragon—oh, I shouldn't do that. Not that it's all that bad, but Amabel's expecting you. Steak and kidney pudding, I believe. Just the right thing for a cold day like this."

"But my luggage—"

"Oh yes, your luggage. You're quite right, we oughtn't to leave it outside. We'll just go round and put in indoors, then come back and have a drink. I think you'll find everything in order in the house. Mrs. Nesbit's invaluable. I think I saw her in there this morning. She may have been putting some flowers there for you. It's the sort of thing she'd do. She's got a key, of course, and she'll come and go without bothering you. You can trust her absolutely. Now just let me get the keys Peter gave me for you."

Fidler vanished abruptly into the house.

A moment later he was back with a small bunch of keys in his hand. However, he did not offer them to Andrew, but kept them in his possession while he ushered Andrew down the garden path and then up Peter's, and had used one of the keys to unlock Peter's door before it appeared to occur to him that it might have been appropriate to let Andrew do this for himself. He had pushed the door open before he held out the bunch to Andrew.

"Here you are—the front door, the back door, and that's the key of the garage and that's the car key," he said. "Not that we bother a great deal about locking up here, but still, as I said, we're on the main road and things sometimes do happen . . . Now where's your luggage? Ah yes." He stooped quickly and picked up Andrew's two heavy suitcases. For a man as plump and soft-looking as Fidler was, he moved surprisingly swiftly and lightly and lifted the cases without any sign of strain. "Now let's go and have that drink. You'd like a drink, wouldn't you? Come along."

The truth was that Andrew felt he would like a drink very much and the thought of a good hot steak and kidney pudding, rather than a snack in a pub, was distinctly appealing. But having said that he would very much enjoy having lunch

with the Fidlers, he added that he would like just to take a
quick look round the cottage before leaving it.

Not that there was anything unfamiliar about it. It was
only a year since he had last spent a week-end there with
Peter, who did not seem to have made any significant
changes since that time. At one end of the living-room, a
quite big room which occupied nearly the whole of the
ground floor and had a small kitchen opening out of it, there
were bookshelves from floor to ceiling. At the other end
there was a small Regency dining-table with chairs of ap-
proximately the same period. There were several easy chairs
and there was a window which took up most of one wall.
There was no fireplace, but a long radiator ran almost from
end to end of the room under the window. On a low table in
front of it there was a big white jug filled with branches of
holly, smothered in scarlet berries. It was a reminder that
Christmas was only ten days away and indicated that Fidler
had been right when he had guessed that that morning Mrs.
Nesbit had brought in, if not flowers, the next best thing that
she could manage to greet the newcomer. The room felt
warm and snug and welcoming.

"Very nice," Andrew said, moving towards the window
and looking out. "I'm going to enjoy being here."

He could see both the little old cottage with the thatched
roof from the window and the red brick Victorian house.

"Who lives there?" he asked, gesturing at the cottage as
Fidler came to stand beside him.

"A young fellow called Simon Kemp," Fidler answered.
"He's the games master at Newsome's. He took the cottage
about a year ago when he got married, but his wife walked
out on him almost at once, no one knows why, and he's
stayed on there ever since, letting the place go pretty much
to pieces. Amabel's sorry for him and does her best to look
after him, but my own belief is he doesn't mean to stay. He's
always talking of going to New Zealand. We've had a good

many changes around here recently. Peter of course doesn't
spend much of his time here any more since he got so successful, and we miss him because we always found him good
company. And we miss the old couple who used to live in
Kemp's cottage. They were real locals, nothing to do with
Newsome's, and they'd been living there for half a century
before we came, but they died, one quite soon after the
other, a couple of years ago. The only people who stay on are
the Goodchilds. They're your neighbours on that side . . ."
He nodded towards the red brick house.

Remembering the tall, exceedingly diffident man who had
appeared on one of his earlier visits to Peter to return a
book, Andrew said, "I think I've met Mr. Goodchild." He
looked out of the window at the charming old house that
faced the row of cottages from the other side of the road.
"And that's Godlingham House, is it?"

"That's right," Fidler said. "Beauty of a house, isn't it? If
I'd any ambitions, and it isn't wise for a schoolmaster to have
ambitions, it would be to live in a house like that. Mrs.
Hewison lives there. She's the sister-in-law of our headmaster. Strange woman. Tragic, really. Been a bit peculiar ever
since her husband's death. You probably won't see anything
of her."

Andrew nearly said, "Ah yes, your murderess," but he
stopped himself just in time.

CHAPTER 2

Andrew enjoyed his lunch with the Fidlers. It was not only that the steak and kidney pudding was exceptionally good and that there was an appetizing selection of cheeses to follow it, but Amabel Fidler turned out to be quite different from what Andrew had been expecting. From the things that her husband had said about her, Andrew had assumed that she would be a domineering, interfering sort of person, probably inclined to talk about good works and to try to get him involved in them. In fact, she was a pretty little woman of about thirty-five with soft fair hair which was rather untidy but nevertheless framed her small face attractively. She had big grey eyes and a gentle voice. The only sign of strength about her were her eyebrows, which were level and dark. Yet Andrew soon perceived that in her presence Jack Fidler was noticeably less self-assertive and far less inclined to interrupt everything that Andrew tried to say. She had a way of looking at him with an amused sort of reproof which appeared to control him.

After sherry in the sitting-room, which was extremely neat, with pale, modern furniture and exuberantly coloured curtains and chair-covers, they drank beer with the meal, then returned to the sitting-room for coffee. But this had barely been poured out when Jack Fidler looked at his watch, exclaimed, "Work! See you later, I hope, Professor," and dashed out.

Amabel looked at her watch and said, "Yes, he's late. There's a staff-meeting, I believe. Luckily the term breaks up the day after tomorrow. It's been a very busy one for him and he's tired. He needs a holiday. Is this a holiday for you, or have you brought work with you? Peter said something to us about a book you're writing."

Andrew told her a little about his book. He did not normally talk about it any more than he could help, particularly to people who had no scientific interest, and he gathered that though her husband taught biology, she had none. Before her marriage, she told him, she had been an assistant matron at Newsome's. But Andrew found himself telling her that he was writing a life of Robert Hooke and when she wanted to know who he was, went on to tell her far more about the man and his work than he usually did. She urged him to go on with little words of encouragement and occasional questions which seemed to indicate genuine interest and it was with a start that he realized that the time was half past three. There was even a tinge of dusk in the grey day.

"Good heavens, I didn't realize how long I'd stayed," he said, getting to his feet in a hurry. "You must forgive me. I'm sure there are all sorts of things you meant to do and I've kept you from them. But it's been so pleasant for me."

"But so it has for me," she answered, smiling.

"I'm sure I've been boring you."

"Far from it. I like people to talk about what interests them. I can't contribute much myself. I've never done anything exciting or outstanding."

"You've at least learnt how to listen very well and that's a rare talent," he said. "Now I must make tracks to the village before it gets too dark. I must do a little shopping there to tide me over till tomorrow."

"I don't really think you need to," she said. "I hope you

don't think it was a liberty, but when you didn't let us know what you'd like stocked in, I thought I'd just get a few things for you. There are eggs and bacon and bread and butter and tea and all that sort of thing. So unless you want to cook yourself something more than that, I don't think you need go out now."

"But that's immensely thoughtful of you." When Jack Fidler had suggested that Amabel should do just what she had done, Andrew had been irritated, as if it had been mere interference, but now that he knew her it felt different. "No, I certainly shan't cook anything to speak of after that delicious pudding. I wish I could ask you and your husband over soon for something half as good, but my cooking is a little primitive. But you must come round for drinks some time when I've got settled in."

"Thank you," she said, going to the door with him, "we'd love that. And you must meet Simon Kemp, our other neighbour. Most of the staff at Newsome's go away once the term is over, but I know Simon's staying on. And so are the Goodchilds, of course. They never go away."

"I believe Mr. Goodchild's retired, isn't he?" Andrew said.

"I suppose so."

It struck Andrew as a slightly odd answer. It seemed to imply that she knew very little about the Goodchilds, although they had been neighbours for several years, and there was a sound of reluctance in her voice, as if she would have preferred not to talk about them at all.

"And Mrs. Hewison—will she be here?" he asked.

Amabel Fidler's face went blank. For a moment she said nothing, but, opening the front door, stood looking out at the house on the other side of the road.

"I don't know," she said. "In any case, I don't suppose you'll meet her."

"A lovely house," Andrew said.

She seemed not to have heard him and with a certain

abruptness said goodbye. Andrew made his way down the steep, slippery garden path and up the path to Peter's cottage.

In fact, he met Pauline Hewison next day.

He had spent an agreeable evening, after unpacking and arranging his books and papers in one of the three rooms on the upper floor, which contained a fair-sized table at which he thought he would be able to write in comfort. From its window, which faced away from the road, he could see the low swell of the downs, not the downs as he remembered them from his childhood, green and smooth with a few sheep grazing on them, but a chequer-board of dark ploughed land and great fields of pale brown stubble. But still there was the old sense of space and quiet about them. Some sea-gulls, that must have come inland for many miles, looking for food, had been wheeling in the wintry sky.

He had hung up his suits in the wardrobe in the bigger bedroom, stowed his other belongings away in drawers there, then had gone downstairs, poured out a stiff whisky for himself, chosen a detective story from the stock on Peter's shelves and settled down to spend a restful evening. At about eight o'clock he had made an omelette from the eggs that he had found in the refrigerator and for which he remembered with annoyance at himself he had not paid Amabel, and after that he had watched the nine o'clock news on television and soon afterwards had gone early to bed. Next morning he woke at about seven o'clock, as he usually did, got up and had a shower, shaved, dressed and went downstairs to make himself some breakfast.

While he was doing this he started singing half-aloud to himself.

> "There was a pig went out to dig
> On Christmas Day, on Christmas Day,
> There was a pig went out to dig
> On Christmas Day in the morning . . ."

He had always talked and sung aloud to himself a good deal, even when Nell had been alive and had sometimes overheard him. It had always embarrassed him if he knew that she had done so, and he had tried to control to a whisper the reciting of the verses with which his head was stocked, but now that he spent most of his time alone he had given up the attempt to do this and chanted them aloud as much as he felt inclined.

It was perhaps unfortunate, he sometimes thought, that so much of what he knew by heart were childish songs and nursery rhymes. In later life he had done his best to augment these with Shakespeare, Milton and Donne, but the simple old rhymes would keep breaking in. His memory of what he had learnt in his early childhood was unfailing, even though now the face and name of someone whom he had met the week before might vanish instantly.

He had brought coffee with him from Fortnum's, feeling fairly sure that whatever else might be obtainable in the excellent village shop, good coffee would not be on its shelves, and while he was making the coffee he ate a small piece of cheese, which was amongst the supplies with which Amabel had filled his refrigerator. Andrew always started the day with a small piece of cheese. At some time he had read that it was a good thing on waking to eat some protein, and though he had an uneasy feeling that this might be only a cranky superstition, which made him half-furtive in the way that he did it, he had adopted the habit, since he could not be bothered to boil an egg, and was sure that he benefited.

By the time that the coffee and the toast were made he was proclaiming,

> "There was a sheep went out to reap
> On Christmas Day, on Christmas Day,
> There was a sheep went out to reap
> On Christmas Day in the morning . . ."

It was the nearness of Christmas, he supposed, that was making it impossible for him to get this agricultural jingle out of his head. Doing his best to quell it, he put his breakfast tray on the table in the sitting-room and was glad to find that Peter had not stopped his newspaper and that a copy of *The Times* had just been delivered.

Drawing back the curtains over the long window, he saw with pleasure that the sky was blue and clear, though there had been a heavy frost in the night. The lawn in front of the house was almost as white as if it had snowed. Hoar-frost crusted the branches of a birch tree at the edge of the lawn. But the room was acceptably warm. Returning to the table, he settled down to enjoy a comfortable breakfast. He had put on old tweed trousers and a favourite cardigan. He was not wearing slippers. He had packed a pair, but generally when he was alone he preferred to walk about in his socks.

He drank three cups of coffee and had read most of what interested him in the newspaper before he thought of moving. By then sunlight, from a sun very low in the sky, had penetrated the room. Carrying his tray out to the kitchen again, he washed up his cup and saucer under the tap and prepared to go out.

His first call, as he had decided that it must be, was on Amabel Fidler to repay her what she had spent on buying his supplies. She asked him if he had found everything that he had needed and if he had slept well, and said in her gentle way that he should let her know if there was anything more that she or Jack could do for him. She had an account of what she had spent and Andrew paid it, thanked her yet again for all that she had done, asked directions to the village shop and set off in very good spirits.

He had brought a shopping-basket with him and though he did not really know what he wanted, he hoped that wandering round the shop would give him some ideas. Amabel had told him that besides the grocer there was a small

butcher in the village, so it seemed to him that except when
he wanted to cash a cheque or go to a chemist he would not
have to drive into Maddingleigh very often.

The way into the main part of the village was along the
road past Peter's cottage and the Goodchilds' red house,
then down a narrow lane on the right, which led to a green
which was surrounded by cottages and bungalows, ancient
and modern, a pub, a church, a village hall and the shops for
which Andrew was seeking. There was a great chestnut in
the middle of the green and a small stream meandered past
it, with a few ducks paddling about in the clear water.

Andrew went first to the butcher, bought some fillet
steaks, some mince and some sausages. That should last him
till well after the weekend, he thought. Then he went to the
grocer, which was a self-service shop and where he helped
himself to a variety of vegetables and the few odds and ends
with which Amabel had not provided him. Then he took his
place in the queue leading to the counter where payments
were made and had nearly reached it when the woman who
was standing in front of him dropped a glove.

He stooped to pick it up. The woman herself stooped at
the same moment and their heads collided.

"I beg your pardon," Andrew said. He had the glove in his
hand before she reached it and, straightening up, he held it
out to her.

"My fault," she answered, taking it. "Thank you."

She turned back to the counter.

"Good morning, Mrs. Hewison," the woman behind it
said. "Nice day, isn't it, though this cold makes my back hurt
something wicked. I've got pills for it—they give you pills for
everything nowadays, don't they?—but they don't do much.
Tea, sugar, salt . . ."

She started emptying the wire basket that had been
placed before her.

Something wicked . . .

The phrase echoed in Andrew's mind as he looked with curiosity at the woman whom he had heard described as probably a murderess, in spite of the fact that she could prove her innocence. A woman at the mention of whose name faces became strangely blank. A woman whom he had been assured he would never meet.

By the pricking of my thumbs,
Something wicked this way comes . . .

Was that what he felt when he saw her?

She was tall and slenderly built, though her shoulders were broad. He judged her to be about forty. Her hair was dark but faintly frosted with grey, parted in the middle and drawn smoothly back from her face into a roll at the back of her head. Her head was small and held high on a graceful neck. As she was standing with her back to him in the queue, he could not see her face, but in the glimpse of it that he had had when he and she had both bent to pick up her glove, he had seen that it had the kind of finely formed features that could stand the severe way that she wore her hair. He had also seen that she wore a good deal of make-up, a high colour on her cheeks, which otherwise would probably have been pale, and a quantity of eye-shadow that made her dark eyes look large and intense. She was wearing a suede jacket and a tweed skirt which looked casual, yet which fitted her too well to have been anything but expensive. But the car in which she drove away from the shop a minute or two later was an old red Mini. As he paid for his groceries Andrew wondered what other car she kept in the garage of her mansion.

He walked home briskly. The road was treacherous with ice and even though he had put up the hood of the quilted anorak that he had brought with him, the air felt sharply cold on his face. But it was exhilarating. He would do a long spell of writing that afternoon, he told himself. His notes for the next chapter of his book were in order and he knew what he wanted to say. He felt eager to work. It seemed to him that he was going to find the change from his flat to Peter's cottage stimulating.

Perhaps, he thought, he ought to look for new surroundings more often than he did. Really he lived in a very sedentary way. He had got into a rut. Since his trip round the world after he had retired he had spent hardly a single night away from St. John's Wood. And there was nothing to keep him there but habit. He must take himself in hand, he decided. Why shouldn't he spend the spring in Italy, for instance? It was years since he had been to Italy. But the trouble was that he had never much enjoyed travel without Nell. Even on that trip round the world, so rewarding in many ways, he had felt at times unbearably forlorn and all the time that something vital was missing.

He was just opposite the gate of the Victorian house when he was accosted by a man who stood there holding a bicycle.

"Good morning," the man said. "I believe you're Professor Basnett."

Andrew recognized him. He was the man whom he had met once before in Peter's cottage, the extremely shy man who had retreated as fast as he could on encountering Andrew, and who Andrew now assumed was Godfrey Goodchild. He was smiling nervously, as if he were deeply uncertain of how his greeting would be received. He looked about sixty. He was a tall, gaunt man, whose thinness, however, did not look natural to him. He gave the impression that he ought to have been well built and muscular, but had somehow inappropriately shrunk to almost bare bones. He had a long, hawk-like face, yellowish in colour, brown hair clipped close to his head and large, melancholy brown eyes behind round spectacles. He was wearing a sheepskin jacket and very old, stained flannel trousers.

"Good morning," Andrew replied and automatically assumed the smile with which he had been in the habit of reassuring very young and diffident students. "Yes, I'm Peter Dilly's uncle and your neighbour for the winter. I think you must be Mr. Goodchild. Peter's spoken of you."

"Yes—yes, I am," the man answered in a tone of faint astonishment, as if he were not merely surprised at Andrew's knowledge of who he was, but at also recognizing this strange fact about himself. "Would you care—that is, if you aren't busy at the moment—I was going to say—well, it would give me and my wife great pleasure—I mean, if you've time to spare—if you would come in for a drink."

"That's very kind of you," Andrew said. "I should love to."

"Now?" the man asked excitedly, as if this were too much to hope for.

"Yes, now or later, if you'd prefer that."

"No, no, now—come in, come in." Godfrey Goodchild swung the gate open. "Peter told us you were coming. He's a great friend of ours. We're both very fond of him. He's a very gifted young man, isn't he? We're so glad he's had such a success."

Once the unnerving experience of offering his invitation was over, the man relaxed a little and spoke with almost incoherent speed.

Andrew walked beside him as he wheeled his bicycle up the path to the house. There was a large basket full of packages fixed to the handlebars.

"I've just been into Maddingleigh, shopping," Goodchild explained. "It's much cheaper there. It's really worth going in. The prices they charge you in the village shop are exorbitant. And as I cycle, of course I don't even have to consider the price of petrol, getting there and back. That's quite a factor nowadays, isn't it? I go in pretty often, so if there's anything you'd like me to pick up for you any time, just let me know."

"Thank you, I will," Andrew said, though he thought it unlikely that he would. Apart from the fact that he was usually reluctant to impose on anyone else's good nature, he rather enjoyed doing his own shopping. "Have you lived here a long time?"

"Nearly twenty-five years. In those days—I mean when we first came here—Peter's cottage and that man Fidler's hadn't been built yet." Godfrey Goodchild did not wheel his bicycle towards the front door of the house, which had a curiously sealed look, as if it were seldom used, but to a door at the side, where he leant the bicycle against the wall and began gathering up his packages into his arms. "Hannah— that's my wife—took on a job as district nurse here for a time, but she found it too much for her and retired some years ago. I hope you don't mind coming in through the kitchen. I generally come in this way. It saves getting mud on the carpets. Now if you'd be so kind as to open that door . . ." He nodded at it and Andrew opened it for him. With his hands full of parcels, Godfrey Goodchild led the way into a large kitchen and dumped what he was carrying on the table in the middle of it. "Hannah!" he called. "Hannah— here's Professor Basnett come to have a drink with us!"

The kitchen was very old-fashioned. It had a deep stone sink and even had a coal range, though this was plainly not in use, for there was an electric cooking-stove, which with the refrigerator looked amazingly out of date in the drab place. Godfrey Goodchild led the way through it to a room at the front of the house. As he and Andrew entered it a man who had been sitting in one of the chairs stood up and Goodchild greeted him, "Ah, Simon."

The man was stocky and heavily built and probably about thirty years old. He had curly fair hair which stood up straight from his forehead, healthy, ruddy cheeks, a snub nose, a square jaw and friendly blue eyes. Goodchild introduced him as Simon Kemp, who lived in the small thatched cottage beyond the Fidlers'. Andrew remembered that Jack Fidler had told him that Simon Kemp was games master at Newsome's.

"We're going to have a drink," Goodchild said, making it sound as if this were an unusual event of some importance. "You'll join us, won't you, Simon?"

"No, Godfrey, thank you, really I must go," Kemp answered. "I only looked in to see if you'd been able to get my library books in Maddingleigh. Hannah said she thought you'd be back any time, so I waited. But I've got to get back to the school. Did you have any luck with my books?"

"I'm sorry, no, no luck," Goodchild said. "But I've put your name down for them." He turned with a smile to Andrew, who realized that when the man smiled you could see the ghost in his ravaged face of someone who had once been very good-looking. "Simon likes books about animals and farming, mostly in far-off places. Australia, New Zealand. I've a feeling we're going to lose him one day to the Antipodes." He went to the door and once more called out, "Hannah!"

Simon Kemp thrust out a large hand to Andrew, but though it looked capable of a bone-crushing grip, fortunately it was gentle.

"Goodbye, Professor. Nice to have met you." He departed in the direction of the kitchen and the back door as footsteps came hurrying down the stairs and Hannah Goodchild came into the room.

She was a small, bustling woman of about the same age as her husband. She had curly grey hair, cut short, so that it made a neat cap on her head, was plump, broad-bosomed and broad-hipped. She was wearing a limp navy blue jersey dress that looked as if it had been through many washes, with a plastic apron over it, and had a duster in one hand.

"Look at the fire!" she exclaimed. "You haven't even lit it, Godfrey. Poor Professor Basnett must be frozen. Good

morning, Professor. You must forgive Godfrey for not looking after you properly. He lives in a world of his own. The
needs of other poor mortals don't get through to him."

The room was indeed very cold. A fire had been laid in the
grate, but had not been lit and there was no other heating. It
was a muddle of a room, furnished mostly with what had
been modern in the 1930s and which had plainly stood a
good deal of battering since that time, but there was not a
speck of dust to be seen or a spot on the faded carpet, which
had an angular pattern of greens and brown which in those
long-ago days would have been called contemporary.

Hannah Goodchild went quickly to the fireplace, struck a
match and held it to the crumpled newspaper in the grate.
For a moment, as the paper seemed reluctant to catch, she
stood watching it dubiously, then as flames appeared and the
first crackling of the kindling was heard, she turned back to
Andrew, smiling at him though she went on talking to her
husband.

"Those drinks, Godfrey. And don't forget the peanuts.
There are still some in the tin on the shelf behind the shoe
polish. I shouldn't bother with those cheesy things—we've
had them rather too long. Is sherry all right, Professor? I'm
afraid it's all we have."

It was not only all that they had, but was of a very sweet
variety which Andrew found faintly nauseous, though when
the Goodchilds asked him anxiously how he liked it he said
that it was excellent. The peanuts had a slight taste of musti-
ness which made him feel thankful that the cheesy things, if
they were of still greater antiquity, had not been produced.
Goodchild served the sherry with a mixture of diffidence
and formality which showed that producing drinks for unex-
pected visitors in this household was not a thing that occurred very often.

"You met Simon just now, didn't you?" Hannah said.
"Such a sad story, but perhaps you've heard it already."

Here we go again, Andrew thought, more gossip. It was beginning to fascinate him. He was accustomed to academic gossip and thought of it as an unavoidable part of life, but he had not been prepared to encounter it here.

"Dear," Goodchild interrupted quickly, "I'm sure Professor Basnett isn't interested. I mean, why should he be? A complete stranger. I really think we should talk of something else."

His wife took no notice of him. "Well, Simon got married, you see," she said. "To the daughter of that awful woman over there." She nodded towards the window, from which Godlingham House could be seen. "Ruth, the girl's name is. That was about a year ago. And it broke up almost at once and she went back to her job in advertising. I've heard she's doing very well in it. I believe they mean to have a divorce, though it's too early for them to be able to get ahead with it, because you can't get a divorce through so quickly after marriage, can you, unless it's a case of gross misconduct—?"

"Dear," her husband said again unhappily, "please—"

She swept on, "Well, of course there wasn't any question of that on either side. I've never liked the girl, she's got too much of her mother in her, but I don't think there was really time for either her or Simon to have done anything too disgraceful. Simon, we know, is a charming boy. Man, I ought to say, but I always think of him as a boy. I'm sure he didn't understand what he was getting into when he married that woman's daughter. So I suppose it was incompatibility, which they'd have found out about if they'd had a longer engagement, but people hardly seem to have engagements at all nowadays. D'you know, I've sometimes wondered if she had another husband all the time, or something like that, and hadn't thought it was important enough to mention it to Simon. What's a little bigamy, after all, compared with some of the things that go on—?"

"Really, Hannah!" her husband interjected more forcibly

than before. "You haven't the slightest evidence for suggesting such a thing."

"Perhaps not *evidence,*" she said. "It's just that I believe in heredity and we know the kind of woman her mother is. It's true we don't know what her father was like, but it's my guess he wasn't much good either."

"Am I right that this girl you're talking about was a daughter of Mrs. Hewison's by a former marriage?" Andrew said. "I mean, not a child of Mr. Hewison's."

She nodded her head several times. "Quite right, except that I don't think you need assume there was ever a former marriage. A child, yes—but a marriage . . ." She gave a scornful laugh.

"Hannah, you must stop this!" Goodchild cried. The way that she had been talking seemed to cause him real pain. There was anxious distress on his long, yellowish face. "Professor, you mustn't take any notice of her. We know nothing whatever against the girl and nothing much against her mother, if it comes to that. She was the victim of a great misfortune. I think we should leave it at that. But the fact is, we're very attached to Simon and we know he was desperately upset when his marriage went on the rocks like that. But it isn't for us to apportion blame. We know nothing about the circumstances. The girl may have had her reasons—"

"My dear, if you're suggesting Simon is *impotent,*" Hannah exclaimed, "I'm sure you're quite mistaken. I mean, look at him. Is it likely?"

"You can't always judge by appearance, but still, I wasn't suggesting anything of the sort," Goodchild replied with agitation. "I've sometimes thought perhaps she thought he'd leave Newsome's and join her in London. I can't see her ever settling down happily here. I sometimes think that's why he keeps reading those travel books he likes me to get from the library. I mean, that he thinks she might come back to him if he moves away. Some more sherry, Professor?"

Andrew hastily refused another glass. He did not stay much longer, but a short time afterwards, carrying the shopping-basket that he had left in the kitchen, made his way home to Peter's cottage.

As he went he thought how strange it was that the solitary woman, living in that peaceful-looking old house on the far side of the road, seemed to dominate the members of the small community in which he found himself and to rouse surprisingly strong emotions in them. Could the real truth be, he found himself wondering, that what these people really had against the woman was that she had not murdered her husband? Could it be that to go on suspecting her, whatever the evidence might be in her favour, gave them a kind of excitement that was missing from their quiet lives? Then he remembered that his nephew seemed to feel the same uneasiness about her and certainly Peter's life was full enough for him not to need that kind of titillation. But his trouble might be an overactive imagination. As Andrew reached his gate and went up the path through the garden to the cottage he began to think that he would like to meet the woman again, though he knew enough about himself to recognize that he would make no effort to do so.

Letting himself into the cottage, he realized at once that there was someone else in it. Someone was softly whistling in the kitchen. The sound broke off as he closed the front door behind him and a woman in an emerald green anorak and black trousers appeared at the kitchen door. She looked about forty-five and had fluffy red hair hanging down in a curly fringe from under a tartan woollen scarf. She had a plump round face, freckles and wide-spaced, pale blue eyes. She held out a hand.

"Good morning, Mr. Basnett," she said. "I'm Mrs. Nesbit.

It isn't my day for coming, but I thought I'd look in as I was passing to make sure everything's all right."

Andrew shook hands with her.

"Perfectly all right," he answered. "Perfectly. Thank you very much indeed for all your help. And particularly for that nice vase of holly."

"Well, I always think flowers or something like that give a place a homely look," she said. "And of course it's nice and warm here. I turned up the thermostat a bit, as it got so cold outside. Cold enough for snow, isn't it? It wouldn't surprise me if we've a white Christmas for once. It sort of makes me remember . . ." She broke off and, reaching for the basket that Andrew was carrying, took it from him and carried it into the kitchen.

"Yes?" he said, following her, his curiosity getting the better of him. "It makes you remember what?"

"Oh, just another bad winter we had some years ago," she answered. "Power cuts and all that, and other troubles too. No need to think about such things now though. Personally I can do without snow. Messy stuff you bring in all over your carpets if you go out in it. Now is there anything I can do for you? You've only to say."

"Nothing—nothing whatever, thank you," he said. "I've found everything very comfortable. Those other troubles you mentioned . . ."

"Oh well, it was just a nasty accident that happened across the way. You don't want to worry about that, it's long ago. Poor Mr. Hewison shot himself while he was cleaning his revolver. At least, that's always been my opinion and I knew Mr. and Mrs. Hewison better than most people. I was their housekeeper in those days before I met Mr. Nesbit and got married. People will tell you all sorts of things about what happened, but that's what I think. Now I'll be off home. I'll be in Tuesday to do my work here, if that's convenient for you. Tuesday's always been my day for Mr. Dilly."

"Splendid," Andrew said. "And thank you again."

"Don't mention it."

As she let herself out, Andrew went into the sitting-room, kicking off his shoes and leaving them lying in the middle of the room, then poured himself out a stiff whisky and settled down with it in the warm, comfortable room to get rid of the taste of the Goodchilds' sherry and peanuts.

On the following Sunday he met Henry Hewison.

In the interval Andrew had not seen any of his neighbours again and he had quickly established a routine of work, more or less the same as his routine at home except that he allowed himself longer for a walk on the downs in the afternoon than he usually did in the streets around the St. John's Wood block of flats. Even so, the walk was not usually very long. The days were so short that if he went a little too far, tempting as it was to do so in the peaceful emptiness of the hills, it would have been very easy to be overtaken by darkness.

The change from London to Godlingham seemed to be doing him good. He was writing freely and with pleasure. He had felt no inclination yet to return the Fidlers' or the Goodchilds' hospitality, though at times he reminded himself that he ought not to wait too long to do this. Then on Sunday morning at about ten o'clock his telephone rang and the headmaster of Newsome's introduced himself. He had a rather high-pitched, neighing voice.

"I was wondering if you'd care to come in for a drink this evening," he said. "Say about half past six. I shall be alone. The school's broken up, of course, and the normal entrance is closed, but there's a side entrance onto a staircase that leads straight up to my flat. I'll see that the light's left on outside the door and if you ring, the caretaker will let you in. I hope you can spare the time. I heard of your being here from Dilly. We miss him, of course, though I can't say I ever felt he was cut out to be a schoolmaster. I think he took to it only because he didn't know what else to do until he found his real vocation."

That was Andrew's opinion about his nephew. He accepted the invitation and was given instructions how to find the school.

These were unnecessary, as only the afternoon before he had paused at its gates and seen the sprawl of buildings of which it was composed. At the heart of them was a fair-sized house, covered in cream-coloured stucco, which was Victorian and belonged to the period when it had been thought proper to ape the Gothic. It had battlements and little turrets and a square tower jutting up at one end of it high above its roof. This, Andrew supposed, was the house that had belonged to the family called Newsome, who had bequeathed the school its name. But other more recent buildings clustered round it. He guessed that they contained laboratories, perhaps dormitories or a library. He could see a football field at one side of them.

The school was at least a mile from Godlingham and sooner than walk that distance in the dark, he decided to take out Peter's car. It was the first time that he had had it out of the garage, so he allowed himself plenty of time to make sure that he could handle it. It was a long time since he had last driven. But he found no difficulties with it and arrived at the school at just about the time for which he had been invited.

He found the door with the light above it and the name H. HEWISON lettered across it and rang the bell. The door was opened by an old, slightly lame man who admitted in a grudging tone that Andrew was expected, indicated a staircase ahead, then disappeared through a door that led, Andrew supposed, into the main school building. Climbing the stairs, he found a man standing at the top of them to receive him.

"Professor Basnett?" The man thrust out a hand. "So good

of you to come. It's very cold, isn't it? Come in and get warm."

He was very tall and very thin, with a small head carried high on a long, thin neck. He had a narrow face with a long chin, which he held pushed forward in a curiously outthrust way, small, pointed ears and heavily lidded eyes behind thick spectacles. Gripping Andrew by the arm, he propelled him into a room where there was a good fire burning, a bright light from some fluorescent tubes close to the ceiling, an astonishing quantity of papers, files and books scattered everywhere and also a number of wooden planks piled up at one end, leaning against what looked like the beginnings of some bookshelves. Two walls of the room were already covered with books, but the existing shelves were apparently insufficient for Henry Hewison's needs and he was having some more made.

"Sit down, sit down," he said, pushing a high-backed leather chair closer to the fire. His voice did not sound as high-pitched as it had on the telephone, but it had a peculiar whinnying note. "Sorry about the mess, but I've at last got round to having a few bookshelves made. Nesbit's making them. The village joiner. Splendid workman. Of course I pay him in cash. The black economy. Not altogether moral, but it means the job doesn't come too expensive and one has to think of that nowadays, doesn't one? Now what will you have to drink? I've all the usual things, I think. Whisky . . . ? Oh dear, I seem to have let that get rather low. Gin? But I'm afraid the tonic may be rather flat. Brandy, of course. Now where's that got to? I was sure I had some. But what about some cherry brandy? Do you care for that? I confess it's my own favourite. Nice and warming in weather like this."

Cherry brandy was not Andrew's favourite drink, but he accepted the singularly small glass of it that he was given.

"Is the Nesbit who's making your shelves any relation of the Mrs. Nesbit who's going to work for me?" he asked.

"Her husband, I believe. Excellent couple. She used to be my brother's housekeeper. Left the job when she got married." Henry Hewison walked to a chair facing Andrew's from the other side of the fireplace. He had an undulating walk, placing his feet delicately on the carpet. All of a sudden Andrew recognized where Peter had found the inspiration for his book *Camellords*. There was no doubt about it, Henry Hewison bore a distinct resemblance to a camel. He had its air of hauteur, its high-held head, its swaying walk. He even had its way, Andrew saw as the man sat down, of rolling his lower jaw slightly, as if he were chewing his cud. His high-pitched voice was not like the camel's grumbling roar, yet there was no doubt about it, he had been Peter's model.

Presently, as they went on to converse, Andrew began to think that it had not been only by his appearance that Henry Hewison had inspired Peter. He soon began to talk about his school. It was unlikely, Andrew thought, that he would ever talk much about anything else. It filled the man's whole horizon. Explaining to Andrew what had led him to start it in the first place, he exclaimed, "Standards! It's become of desperate importance to protect our educational standards. Don't you agree? Once lost sight of, you know, they'll be gone for good, like so many other things. We'll never measure up to them again. And they're being assailed on every side. Don't think I'm decrying the comprehensive schools. They do the best they can with the money and the material they've got. But how can they foster real talent? How can they mould character? Unless some of us who care about such things take a stand before it's too late, the highest level we can achieve will get lower and lower, while the lowest level doesn't get any higher. Not that a place like Newsome's can ever be anything but a drop in the bucket, but still I assure you that the boys who pass through our hands have been given the best that's possible to us, and other people may learn from us in time. We may make mistakes. No doubt we do. We really know very little about the educative process. Everything we do is an experiment and the only result we ever see of our endeavours is the type of young man who goes out into the world from us here, and as we've only been at it for ten years we haven't had much opportunity yet of observing how they turn out."

"But you believe they'll be a kind of élite," Andrew said. He thought of the Camellords and the way in which they had soon dominated mankind. But he found it difficult to believe that anyone educated by this rather mild-seeming man who let his tonic go flat and mislaid his brandy would ever turn out very dominant. Nice, perhaps, and well-meaning and absent-mindedly cultured, but not lordly, as Peter had portrayed them. "You think it's necessary to have one?"

"Well, isn't it?" It sounded as if Henry Hewison had never questioned that. "But it's a new kind we need. The kind that the conventional public schools produce were meant originally to govern an empire. Now we need something quite different. We need men who can cope with industry, with technology, yet have an understanding of the humanities, and have grown up in an atmosphere of freedom. But the tragedy is, we shall never know how we've succeeded. If we have succeeded. To be honest with you, I'll be surprised if we can keep the place going for another year."

"Financial problems?" Andrew asked.

"What else? Naturally we've never had any government grants and the amount of money I was able to put into the place at the beginning, what with inflation, now looks ridiculously small. I had the good fortune to inherit what I thought of as a vast fortune from an aunt of mine, and I believed I could create the kind of school I had always believed in. It was a subject on which I had the most passionate feelings. I had spent my own childhood in a peculiarly dreary school where I was intensely unhappy, then I had become a teacher of history in an equally unenlightened place, so when the shower of gold descended on me I had no doubt at all about what I wanted to do with it. Help came to me almost at once from a number of directions. Many of the parents of children who have been through our hands have helped to create a trust fund to support us. But the truth is, the amount is ludicrously inadequate and somehow I have to face the fact that we shall have to close down soon. I can't tell you what despair I feel at the thought, but it has to be faced. Of course, if my brother had lived, the situation would have been different. He promised me . . . But I'm talking too much about myself and my problems. I must be boring you. Let me give you a little more cherry brandy."

"No, thank you, I have to drive home," Andrew said, though he could not have felt soberer and could have drunk several more of the small glasses without feeling it. "Your brother, I believe, used to live at Godlingham House."

"Ah, you've heard the story," Henry Hewison said. "Yes, poor Charles, we'll never know what really happened that night, though I've ideas of my own . . . However, I shouldn't go into that. I realize it's most unlikely that we'll ever know the truth, though I'll admit to you in confidence that I've never given up the hope of being able to sort the thing out some day. Someone will make a mistake. Some clue will be dropped . . ." His jaw worked gently as he gazed ruminatively into the distance beyond Andrew's head.

"Then you don't believe in the theory that it was simply a break-in," Andrew said.

"Good gracious, no. Never believed in it for a moment. No, I'm fairly sure who did it and why. The only question is, how? It seems impossible, yet there must be a way . . . Did I mention that my brother was going to invest a great deal of

money in Newsome's? He was actually telling me so on the
telephone when something interrupted him and we were
cut off. And he died almost immediately afterwards before
he'd had time to arrange it and his wife inherited all he had.
She's a very rich woman. And she didn't feel any obligation
to carry out what she knew were his wishes, and legally, of
course, she was entirely within her rights. There was nothing on paper. And the truth is that even if Charles had made
over to us what he'd promised, it would only have tided us
over for a short time. All the same, in a short time what may
happen? You never know. Times change. Governments
change. Economic conditions change . . . I sometimes allow myself to have daydreams of what might have happened if poor Charles had lived . . . I do wish I could tempt
you to another cherry brandy. I'm so enjoying our talk."

Most of the talking, Andrew thought, had been done by
his host. It was about eight o'clock when he reached home
and fried sausages for his supper. Next day saw him back at
work while he tried to make up his mind when to make a
trip to London. Not till after Christmas, he thought. It fell on
the next Sunday and there was no point in thinking of travel-
ling for a day or two after it. But possibly the following
Thursday would be a suitable day. On the other hand, perhaps it would be best to wait until after the New Year. He
went for his usual walk in the afternoon and spent the evening watching a television comedy which he felt he ought to
scorn, but to which in reality he was much addicted.

Contrary to Mrs. Nesbit's prophecy, it was not a white
Christmas. She had come in, as she had promised, on the
Tuesday morning before it, bringing with her a large Christmas card for Andrew, depicting a stage-coach apparently
stuck in snow, which he added to the number the porter in
St. John's Wood had forwarded to him from his flat and with
which he was decorating the sitting-room. Mrs. Nesbit went
through the house with a speed and efficiency that staggered

Andrew, leaving it spotless. As a Christmas present to her, he doubled her wages and she promised that she would come again the following Tuesday. The weather had turned mild and clammy. There was heavy rain in the night and when he set off for his usual afternoon walk on the downs the paths were so muddy that he wished it had occurred to him to bring gumboots with him.

The Fidlers invited him to join them at their Christmas dinner. As Andrew walked up to their cottage he reflected what a curious thing it was that people to whom Christmas was a purely pagan festival without any religious significance should still feel they must not let their fellow men spend it alone. For three hundred and sixty-four days of the year they might be left to endure continuous loneliness without interruption, but on the three hundred and sixty-fifth day they must be welcomed in and substantially fed.

The Fidlers' dinner was very substantial and very well cooked. There was a turkey and then a flaming pudding, with champagne cocktails before the meal, burgundy to go with it, then port to go with the nuts and raisins. Andrew was not the only guest. Simon Kemp was there too. The atmosphere was relaxed and contented. They took their time getting through the meal. When at last they got up from the table, with Amabel refusing to let anyone help with the washing-up and bringing coffee into the sitting-room, the afternoon was already showing the first signs of dusk.

Switching on lights, she went to the window and was about to draw the curtains across it when she paused, looking out.

"There aren't any lights on over there," she said. "I suppose Pauline's all alone."

"Her own fault, isn't it, if she is?" Fidler said. "We've asked her here often enough. If she doesn't want to have anything to do with us, that's her look-out."

"As a matter of fact, she isn't alone," Kemp said with a

touch of embarrassment in his voice. "She's got Ruth with her."

"Ruth?" Amabel said, turning to look at him. Then she turned back to the window and drew the curtains. "Have you seen her, Simon?"

"Just in the road yesterday," he answered. "That's how I know she's here. She hasn't been to see me, if that's what you mean."

"I just wondered . . ."

"No," he said, "don't. That's all finished."

His colour had heightened and, like Amabel, Andrew found himself wondering if the marriage was as finished as all that, and whether it was or not, how deep the hurt of what had happened went with the young man. But there was no more talk about it. They fell back on the safest of all topics, their plans for their summer holidays, about which nothing in the least disturbing can ever be said.

It seemed to Andrew as he walked home presently that a bite was back in the air, as if the temperature had dropped several degrees since the morning. That evening he ate a boiled egg and a piece of toast and listened to a Brandenburg Concerto on Peter's hi-fi. In the morning, as usual, he woke at seven o'clock, when there was no light in the room yet and the windows, from which he always drew the curtains back before going to bed, were squares of blackness. Yet he felt a sense as if there were movement outside them. Getting up, he went to one and put his face close to the glass. In spite of the darkness, he could see that it was snowing heavily.

CHAPTER 3

Andrew had his shower and got dressed, went downstairs, ate his little piece of cheese, made coffee and toast and carried it into the sitting-room. Because it was Boxing Day there was no newspaper. Daylight came gradually, made murky by the steadily falling snow. The flakes were very fine, almost a haze against the heavy sky, but the green of the lawn had already disappeared under a crust of white. The birch tree at the edge of it was a gaunt white skeleton. The path to the gate was obliterated.

When he had finished his breakfast, Andrew went to the front door and looked out. There was only a slight wind, yet the snow had drifted against the door and when he opened it a few clots spilled in on the floor inside. But it was not really as cold as it looked and as he presently peered out of the window it seemed to him that the sky was growing lighter and the veil of snow less dense. By ten o'clock it had stopped falling. The clouds had disappeared and the sky had become a faint clear blue. There was a sparkle in the air that made the snow glitter and made Andrew feel that he would have liked to go for a tramp through the shallow but still unsullied whiteness if only he had had the sense to bring gumboots.

If it had not been Boxing Day he would have got out the car and driven into Maddingleigh to buy a pair, but naturally today and probably tomorrow also all the shops would be

closed. The drive itself would not have been difficult. While
he was at the window he saw several cars pass, going to or
coming from the village, and although they moved slowly
and cautiously, they did not seem to be experiencing much
trouble. But the snow was deep enough to stop Andrew
venturing out in his ordinary shoes. It would spill into them
before he reached the gate and he did not relish the thought
of a walk, however exhilarating, in sodden socks. So there
was nothing for it but to settle down to some work.

Once absorbed in it he forgot the snow and although by
the late afternoon, when he drew the curtains over the big
window and shut out the pale white gleam, there was no
sign of a thaw, his only concern was whether or not it would
stop Mrs. Nesbit coming to clean up the cottage next day.
Tomorrow was Tuesday, her day for coming. Not that it
would worry him too much if she felt that she could not face
the walk and did not come. The cottage looked very clean to
him. A little dust here and there really did not seem important. In fact, it gave the place a rather pleasant, lived-in
feeling.

However, Mrs. Nesbit appeared punctually at nine o'clock
next morning. She had on fur-lined boots and was in her
black trousers and emerald green anorak with its hood
pulled up over her head. There had been no more snow in
the night, but there had been a frost and it was a good deal
colder than it had been the day before. She warned Andrew
that it was very slippery outside and advised him not to go
out.

"I nearly had a good fall, coming," she said as she changed
out of her boots into a pair of pink bedroom slippers that she
had brought with her, "and I saw cars in the village skidding
all over the place. There'll be more snow coming, it said on
the forecast. Not that you can believe them. They get it
wrong more often than not. But you can't help listening to

them somehow, can you, and thinking they must know something?"

She hung up her anorak and got to work.

Andrew himself did not attempt to work while she was in the cottage. Apart from the sound of the vacuum cleaner, with which she went into every corner of it, she liked to whistle as she worked and the walls were not thick enough and the noise was too distracting for concentration to be possible. At half past ten he made a second pot of coffee, brought a packet of biscuits out of a cupboard and went to the bottom of the stairs and called up them, "Mrs. Nesbit, I've made some coffee."

She had been cleaning the bath. After a moment she came downstairs, drying her hands on a cloth.

"Now that's really nice," she said. "Just what I was wanting. Just right in this weather. Not that you can feel the cold in here with the lovely heating, and of course working always warms you up. But I do like a cup of coffee. D'you know what I was thinking, Mr. Basnett?"

Andrew disclaimed any knowledge of it. He had poured out two cups of coffee and, feeling companionable, had sat down at the kitchen table.

"I was looking out of the bathroom window at that house over there," Mrs. Nesbit said, taking a chair facing him, "and I was thinking about the way I got stuck in Maddingleigh the night Mr. Hewison died. If that hadn't happened, I mean, if the bus had been able to get through the snow, he might be alive today. Every time we've had snow since then I think about it, but of course we've never had such a blizzard as we had that day. I can't remember the village ever being cut off since that time. It's quite strange how it happened really. If I'd come on the earlier bus I'd have been there and perhaps I could have stopped him."

"I'm sure you've nothing to blame yourself for, if that's been worrying you," Andrew said. "You couldn't help the

blizzard. But do you believe he killed himself? From what
you said before I gathered you thought it was an accident.
Do you think he had any reason for wanting to kill himself?"

"Not what you'd call a *reason*," she answered. "Not that I
know of. I used to hear them quarrelling sometimes, but I
don't know what about. Honestly I didn't listen when I
heard them at it, I'm not like that. But she'd a sharp temper
if she didn't get what she wanted, and he was a stubborn sort
of man. I used to think what she wanted was to get away
from here. I thought we were too quiet for her. And he was
all set to stay, because he'd got interested in that school of his
brother's. I know that's one of the things they used to fight
about."

"Yet Mrs. Hewison's stayed on here all these years since
her husband's death," Andrew said, "so she can't really have
wanted to leave. And what happened to the gun?"

"I don't know. Well, it was just a feeling I had. I may have
been quite wrong. There's a lot about it I never understood.
That business about the casserole, for instance."

"The casserole? What was that?"

"Well, because it was my day off, you see, I'd made a
chicken casserole and left it in the oven. And I'd set the
timer—you know what I mean, the thing you set on an
electric cooker that switches the oven on and off when you
want it—well, I'd set the timer so that it would go on at half
past six and switch off at eight. That was so that it should be
all ready for Mrs. Hewison to dish up when she got home
from her bridge game with the Fidlers. She generally went
out on a Saturday about half past four to have tea with Mrs.
Fidler—they were great friends in those days, though I don't
think they see much of each other now—then she'd come
home about eight to have dinner with Mr. Hewison. And I
generally came home on the bus that passes here about ten
in the evening, only that day I nearly came in the afternoon,
when the snow began, in case there was trouble later about

getting through, and if only I had . . ." She gave a sigh and drank some coffee. "I've a married sister in Maddingleigh and I spent most of my afternoons off with her until I got married myself."

"About the casserole . . ." Andrew said.

"Yes, well, you see, there it was in the oven," she went on, "with nothing for Mrs. Hewison to do when she got home but take it out of the oven and dish it up. Then the snow began. I think it was about half past three it started and it was terrible, like I said, much worse than we've ever had it since. And presently Mr. Porter—he's my brother-in-law—got home from work and he told me the road to Godlingham was cut off and the busses couldn't get through. So I thought I ought to phone Mr. Hewison, who I thought would be at home, that I was stuck in Maddingleigh and couldn't get back till the morning. I think it was soon after five I did that, say about a quarter past. And I didn't get any answer. The police say now it was because he was dead already, but at the time I was just puzzled, because it wasn't like him to go out in that sort of weather. So I thought about it and after a little while I thought the best thing would be to phone Mrs. Fidler and see if I could speak to Mrs. Hewison there. For one thing, I wanted to be sure she understood about the casserole. I hadn't told her anything about having made it before I left. So I phoned and Mrs. Fidler answered, but I'd barely said who I was and asked could I speak to Mrs. Hewison when Mr. Fidler took the phone over from her—you know that way he has of interrupting you whatever you try to say —and he asked what I wanted. So I said again who I was and could I speak to Mrs. Hewison and he said couldn't I give a message for her, because she was playing—well, what is it you play when you're playing bridge three-handed? I don't play bridge myself."

"I suppose she was playing dummy," Andrew said, "though he'd have been playing a hand in the game himself.

I believe Mr. Henry Hewison would normally have been there and there'd have been four of them, but he didn't come, so I've been told, because of the snow."

"That's right. Well, I gave Mr. Fidler the message. I said would he tell Mrs. Hewison I couldn't get back because of the snow, but I'd do my best to get back in the morning, and I said would he tell her there was a casserole in the oven and it'd be ready and would switch itself off at eight o'clock. And he said he'd be sure and tell her just what I said and he rang off. And then there was the power cut. We get a good deal of them round here, I couldn't say why, but usually they don't last for more than an hour or two, but that time it lasted two days. Luckily we'd one of those gas camping-stoves at Godlingham House and I was able to cook quite well on that, and there was an old oil-lamp and plenty of candles in a cupboard and of course there were coal fires, so we weren't too badly off. But I remember Mr. Dilly had a nasty time of it in this house. It's lovely and easy to look after most of the time, but you do depend on the electricity, don't you?"

"I believe my nephew bought himself a portable gas heater after that experience," Andrew said.

"That's right, he did," Mrs. Nesbit said. "It's out in the garage, but I don't think he's ever actually needed to use it. Let's hope you don't either."

"About that casserole . . ."

"Yes, well, you see, it never got cooked. I think the power went off about twenty minutes to six. I'm not sure exactly when it was because of being in Maddingleigh, where they didn't have the cut, but I think it was about then, so the oven never switched itself on. But the funny thing was, when I got back next day after the snow-plough had been along, there the casserole still was in the oven, just as I left it."

Andrew gave a puzzled frown. "I don't see what's funny about that. You mean it was peculiar Mrs. Hewison hadn't taken it out of the oven and perhaps cooked it on the gas camping-stove?"

"Well, wasn't it?"

"I don't know. Of course you know her better than I do, but if you think of what happened that evening after she got home, doesn't it seem probable she simply forgot the casserole? She got back and found her husband dead, didn't she? And I suppose the police came and there was no end of trouble. Do you think she'd have troubled about food?"

"The police couldn't get through till next morning, after the road was cleared. The Maddingleigh police, that's to say. That Superintendent Somebody—I forget his name—and all the others, the photographers and the fingerprint men and all of those—they arrived about nine o'clock. Of course Mr. Grace, the constable in the village, managed to walk up through the snow and so did Dr. Bell, but that was all."

"All the same, coming home and finding your husband shot might take the edge off your appetite," Andrew said.

"Yes." She sounded dubious.

"You don't think so?"

"It's just that she had quite a good meal that evening. She cooked some bacon and eggs and made herself some coffee. I found the things in the sink next morning, so I knew just what she'd had. I know bacon and eggs would have been much easier and quicker to cook on the gas stove than the casserole, but still, just to forget and leave it in the oven . . . The fact is, it wasn't like her. She was always very particular and wouldn't stand waste. I used to think she must have been really poor at some time in her life, because she always knew if I threw away the smallest bits of left-overs instead of somehow making them up. So leaving the chicken in the oven, when for all we knew the power would come on at any moment, though actually it didn't, and the oven might have switched itself on in the middle of the night or any time— well, as I say, it wasn't like her."

"What did the police say when you told them all this?" Andrew asked.

"Oh, I didn't tell them," she said.

"You didn't say anything about it?"

"No."

"Why was that?"

She stirred uneasily. "The fact is, I didn't think anything about it at the time. Like you said, I thought she'd had too much on her mind to remember the casserole. And I expect that's the truth. It'd be natural, wouldn't it? Yes, I'm sure it's the truth."

"Yet there's something worrying you."

"It's only that later on I started to wonder . . ." She wrinkled her forehead in what looked like a painful effort at thought.

"Yes?" Andrew said.

"Well, did she ever get that message I gave to Mr. Fidler?" she asked.

"You mean you wonder if he forgot to give it to her."

"That's it."

"Was she surprised that you didn't get home that night? He was to tell her that, wasn't he?"

"No, she didn't seem surprised. But she could have guessed what happened about that when she heard from someone the road was blocked. But perhaps . . ." She paused again.

"Perhaps she wasn't there in the Fidlers' home when Mr. Fidler said she was. Perhaps that alibi he and Mrs. Fidler gave her was a fake. So you don't really believe in your own theory that Mr. Hewison's death was an accident."

She stood up quickly, gathering up their two coffee-cups and taking them to the sink.

"I'm wasting time, sitting here talking like this," she said. "I must get on. I haven't done the little bedroom yet."

After swiftly washing up the cups, she went back to her work upstairs.

Andrew went to the front door and looked out at the world under its white fleece. Gumboots or not, he decided, he would go for a walk in the afternoon, at least if the sky retained its brightness. Up on the downs the far-spreading white world, pallidly gleaming, should be wonderful. When Mrs. Nesbit had gone and he had heated up a can of soup and eaten some bread and cheese and an orange, he put on his anorak and the heaviest shoes that he had brought, took a walking-stick of Peter's that he had found in a cupboard under the stairs and set out vigorously into the bitter cold.

In the lane that led up to the downs there were no signs of tyre tracks. No car had attempted to go up that day. But there was a track of footsteps clearly trodden into the crisp snow ahead of him, though how long ago they had been made there was no way of guessing. Walking was not easy. It was not that it was slippery, but as he took each step his feet sank a little way into the snow and had to be lifted upwards before he could progress. He had been walking for three quarters of an hour and had begun to think of turning back before he saw the figure ahead of him.

At first sight he was not sure if it was a man or a woman. It was someone tall and slender, wearing a duffle-coat, trousers and boots. Whoever it was seemed, like him, to be thinking of returning to the village, for as Andrew ploughed on, this person stood still, hands in pockets, gazing around at the smooth white loneliness of the hills, then turned and seemed about to start back.

When that happened he realized that it was a woman. Under a brightly coloured woollen cap with a bobble on top, she had dark hair that fell down to her shoulders. Not that long hair nowadays is in itself a proof of femininity, but there was something about the way it curled about her face that looked too attractively deliberate to belong to the long-haired tribe of men. She started when she saw Andrew, seemed to hesitate as if uncertain whether to stay where she was or to go on as before, perhaps in sudden fear at being overtaken by a stranger in this emptiness, then came walking slowly towards him.

When they were only a yard or two apart she stood still and said, "You're Professor Basnett, aren't you?"

He stood still too. "Yes," he said.

"I'm Ruth Kemp," she said. "Or Ruth Hewison. Or Ruth Hockley. Whichever name you prefer."

He recognized then her resemblance to the woman whom he had encountered briefly in the village shop. She had the same small head and slender neck, the same dark eyes and delicate features. But her colour was her own and the intensity of her gaze owed nothing to eye-shadow. What puzzled Andrew was her age. He had judged the woman in the shop to be about forty and he thought that this girl must be at least twenty-five. She had a look of poise that is seldom to be seen in the very young.

As she saw some bewilderment in his face, she said with something sardonic in her tone, "You're looking as if you've heard of me."

"I believe you must be the wife of Simon Kemp," he said.

"Technically, that's correct," she said. "We aren't divorced yet. And in the mean time I can't make up my mind what to call myself. I've decided that once the divorce has gone through I shall revert to using my real name, which is Hockley. My mother would like me to call myself Hewison, but that was only my stepfather's name and I've never felt really comfortable using it."

"You're Mrs. Hewison's daughter, are you?" he said. "The Mrs. Hewison who lives at Godlingham House."

"Do you know of any other Mrs. Hewison?"

"Well, no, I don't."

"So of course that's who I am. And you're Peter Dilly's uncle, aren't you?"

"Yes."

"Is it true that he's spending the winter in Paris?"

"Yes. That's how it came about that I borrowed his cottage."

"How is he?"

"Very well, so far as I know."

"And writing another book, I suppose." She took a hand out of the pocket of her coat and gestured at the way that they had both walked up the hill. "Shall we turn back?"

"I was thinking of that myself," he said. "It's hard work, walking up here."

They began walking down the hill again, side by side.

"I love Peter, you know," she said. "I really do. He's a dear little man. If only he'd been a few inches taller I'd have married him. Do you think it's terrible for a woman to be as tall as I am?"

He looked her up and down. "I don't think you're six feet," he said. "That's nothing nowadays for a young woman who's been fed on all the right vitamins from birth."

"I take size nine in shoes."

"I don't really know what that signifies. Is it very large?"

"That's in American sizes, of course. In English sizes it would be simply enormous."

"I see." He took nine and a half himself in English sizes and did not know anything about the subtle difference between them and the American. "Are you here on a holiday?"

"Yes, just until the New Year. I live in London. I've a nice flat in Kensington. My mother bought it for me though I could have paid for it myself if I'd got a mortgage. Actually, I'd have preferred to do that."

"I believe you work in advertising."

"Yes, though I haven't got very far up the ladder yet. I'm

pretty much of a novice. All the same, I'm doing quite well. Tell me about Peter. He's an orphan, isn't he?"

"He's been an orphan a long time," Andrew said. "His mother, my sister, and his father were killed in a car accident when he was ten."

"And did you bring him up?"

"Oh no, he went to live with his father's brother and his wife. It was they who looked after him and very good to him they were too."

"But you did a great deal for him, didn't you?"

"Not so very much. I contributed a certain amount to his education, that's all."

"But he always speaks of you as if you're his favourite relative."

"Well, that only came about after he grew up. To tell the truth, I'm not much good with children. But from about the time he became a student he and I became very good friends. I'm very attached to him."

She nodded thoughtfully. She was striding along beside him, her long legs making nothing of keeping in step with him.

"I sometimes see him in London, you know," she said. "Not down here. It would make people talk even more than they do already. I suppose you've heard the sort of thing they say about my mother."

"A certain amount, yes." But he turned his head away from her as he said it. He did not want to discuss the matter with the woman's daughter.

"I suppose you know who's at the bottom of it," she said.

He had a suspicion that it might be Hannah Goodchild. Of all the people whom he had met since he had come here, she had seemed to have the most virulent dislike of Pauline Hewison. But he only shook his head. "I've no idea."

"It's H.H.—my stepfather's brother," she said. "That awful old headmaster. Have you met him yet?"

"Briefly. I had a drink with him a few days ago."

"And didn't he tell you my mother was a murderess?"

"Not that I remember—no, he certainly didn't."

"Well, he will, sooner or later. He can't forgive her, you see, for inheriting all my stepfather's money. He thought he was going to get his hands on it himself for that absurd school of his. He sank all his own money in it, being the idiotic sort of creature he is, and now he's got hardly a penny and the school is going to have to fold up soon because there's no money to keep it going. I believe the fees are enormous, but they don't bring in half of what he needs. And so he goes on hoping he'll somehow be able to prove my mother shot his brother, because I believe you can't benefit financially by a crime you've committed, and if he could pull that off he'd get the lot, as next of kin. I'm not kin at all, of course. Not that it matters to me. I like standing on my own feet."

"Size nine."

She chuckled. She had an attractive laugh with a youthful bubble in it. "I see why Peter likes you."

"Something I can't understand," he said, "why does your mother go on living here if the people around her won't let that old tragedy be forgotten."

"I wish I knew," she said.

"You don't?"

"Oh no. I've tried over and over again to get her to move away and she always says she will and then she does nothing about it. I've often thought it sort of odd. Do you think perhaps her heart's broken and she simply doesn't care any more?"

"I haven't met her yet, except for a moment, that's to say, in the village shop, so I shouldn't like to hazard a guess."

"But do you think hearts do get broken sometimes, or is that all a myth?"

Andrew remembered the time when, in his first loneliness after Nell's death, he had thought his own heart was broken, and when, if he had not had work to keep him going, he might have considered more seriously than he did the overdose of pills that for a long time had seemed tempting. But though in the end, after a fashion, the wound had healed, he had always been conscious of scar-tissue.

"I expect you know as much about it as I do," he said. "It's a disease of youth as much as of old age."

She gave him a sidelong look and her face seemed to close, as if he had said something that had hurt or even angered her. He thought that perhaps she had taken it as an indirect comment on the way that she had treated her husband. She walked on in silence and when she spoke again it was only to say that the snow was very beautiful here, but that it would be horrid in London, dirty and slushy, with cars splashing it all over you as you walked along. But she added with abrupt emphasis that she could never think of living anywhere but in London. When they reached the gates of Godlingham House she thrust out a firm hand to shake his and said how much she had enjoyed talking to him, then went striding up the drive towards the house.

Andrew went on to Peter's cottage. Kicking off his shoes, he left them lying just inside the door, where the snow caked on to them would not do too much damage as it melted, then he padded into the kitchen in his socks to make himself a cup of tea.

It was interesting, he thought, that although the girl had talked to him for a time with almost intimate candour, she had said nothing of her husband. Was it possible, he wondered, that Peter had had something to do with the breakup of that marriage? She seemed to feel a little more than mere curiosity about him, and Peter, Andrew suddenly remembered, had a way of being attracted by girls much taller than himself. But he had always been careful not to become involved in any way in Peter's sex life, which he believed often became dramatic and complicated. He made the tea, took it into the sitting-room, found an Agatha Christie on one of Peter's bookshelves which he believed he had never read before and, as the early dusk closed in, settled down to enjoy a quiet evening. Not that it mattered much if he had read the book before. During the last year or two his memory had become so unreliable that he could read a book over and over again with undiminished enjoyment.

He had decided to go to London on Thursday morning to do some more reading on Robert Hooke in the Royal Society library. By that time there had been no thaw, but the snow on the main road to Maddingleigh had been gravelled and he knew that the drive to the station would not be difficult. He had just put on his overcoat and stocked his briefcase with the papers that he would need for the day and was about to go out to the garage when the telephone rang.

He immediately felt sure that if he answered it he would miss his train, though in fact he had allowed himself more than enough time to catch it. For a moment he had an inclination to let the bell ring unanswered, but its insistent demand defeated him, as it nearly always does with everyone, for there is always the possibility that just that call might be the most important call in one's lifetime. Muttering irritably, he went to the telephone and picked it up.

"Good morning," a high-pitched, neighing voice said. "This is Henry Hewison. You had a nice Christmas, I hope."

"Very nice, thank you," Andrew answered, adding courteously, "And you?"

"Oh yes, thank you. Alone, you know. That's what I prefer now. I used to enjoy spending it with my brother and his wife when he was alive, but since his death I've always found it difficult to be sociable at this season. It still evokes memories that are very painful. And to tell the truth, I'm always glad when it's all over, when the shops open normally and the post and one's newspaper come regularly and one can clear all those Christmas cards out of the way and get ahead with everyday life. But I was going to ask you, would it be convenient if I dropped in on you for a little while this afternoon? There's a matter I'd very much like to discuss with you. I've received some rather curious information and what I need at the moment is a chance to discuss it with someone whose approach to it would be dispassionate. If you would allow me to come and talk it over with you I should be most grateful."

"Unfortunately it happens I'm just leaving for London," Andrew said. "Could we make it some other time? I'd be very glad to see you and to help if I'm able."

"You're going to London—to stay for some time?" Henry Hewison asked anxiously.

"Oh no, just for the day," Andrew answered. "I'm planning to come home quite early—on the three-fifty, actually. I think that gets into Maddingleigh at four forty-five. That means I should be home by say five-fifteen at the latest. If that isn't too late for you, would you care to look in on me then?"

"Five-fifteen—that's excellent. Thank you so much. Suppose we say I'll come about five-thirty. That was about the time I was thinking of suggesting in any case. I think that with your clear mind and detachment from the situation you may be able to give me some valuable help, though I realize that it's imposing on you. But I'm most grateful."

He rang off and Andrew hurried out to the garage as fast as he could.

When he arrived at Maddingleigh station he had twenty-five minutes to wait for his train. There was nothing unusual about that. He always arrived at stations in a mood of breathless haste about half an hour before his train was due. He filled in the time this morning by buying a copy of the *Financial Times* and drinking a cup of what British Railways call coffee. In the train to London, when it arrived, he read

the *Financial Times* with care, trying to discover whether
his modest investments had risen or fallen in value since he
had looked into the matter last, but he could not pretend to
himself that he really understood finance. When it came to
buying or selling stocks and shares he always followed without question the advice of his solicitor and found on the
whole that this worked out fairly well. From time to time he
made small profits on which he did not have to pay any tax
and what could any reasonable man ask for more than that?

At intervals during the journey he thought about Henry
Hewison and what his reason might be for wanting to call
that evening, and hoped that it had nothing to do with the
murder of his brother. It would not have occurred to Andrew that that was what it might be if he had not had the
talk that he had had with Ruth Hockley, as she apparently
liked to be called, up on the downs. She had told him that
her step-uncle, if that was the right way of describing his
relationship to her, was at the bottom of the talk about her
mother and the possibility that she had murdered her husband. Andrew felt that he had already heard enough on that
subject. Leaning back and closing his eyes, he did his best to
dismiss it and to concentrate on Robert Hooke.

On the whole he had a good day. He worked steadily
through the morning, then as he was going to lunch he met a
man who had been the very first Ph.D. student whom Andrew had ever had. The man was now a professor in a Scot-
tish university and had recently been made a Fellow of the
Royal Society and, instead of the rosy-cheeked youth whom
Andrew remembered, was middle-aged and grey-haired.
There is nothing like the ageing of people much younger
than oneself, Andrew thought, for making one feel really
old. However, they discussed the development of enzymes
on growing systems, a subject in which he had managed to
interest the young man years ago, and it had been enjoyable
and somehow cheering to find that something that he had

SOMETHING WICKED

done when he had been young himself had stimulated something of considerable importance in this really very talented man.

After lunch they parted and Andrew went back to work. He was thinking of packing up and going out to look for a taxi to take him back to Paddington when it suddenly occurred to him that the room had become surprisingly dark. But it was not, as he thought for a moment, that he had forgotten to keep an eye on the time and was certainly going to miss his train. Looking out of the window, he saw that it was snowing heavily.

What hope would there be in the circumstances, he wondered, of getting a taxi? Not very much. Packing his papers into his briefcase and fetching his overcoat, he went out into the street. It happened that he was in luck. Almost at once a taxi arrived to deposit a passenger at the entrance to the building behind him and he was able to jump into it ahead of someone who had been standing there longer than he had and who waved at it disconsolately with an umbrella. When Andrew told the driver that he wanted to be taken to Paddington, the man started to grumble to himself as if he had private reasons for objecting to going there, of all places in the metropolis, but his real trouble, Andrew concluded, as he was safely delivered at the station, was a grudge against the kind of life he had to lead, against winter, and particularly against having to drive in blinding snow. In that Andrew sympathized with him. It was not only that great snowflakes had kept heaping themselves on the windscreen, almost defeating the swinging backwards and forwards of the windscreen wipers, but a violent wind had arisen, which whirled the snow straight at the driver's face. Already the cars and busses that surged slowly along the streets had a crust of snow on them and the sky was very dark, as if it had plenty more to deliver.

It would not have surprised Andrew if his train had been

delayed a long time at Paddington. He knew that such a strong and sudden blizzard had a way of disrupting all traffic. But the train crept out of the station on time, and though it seemed to him, looking out at the lights that he could see from the window, that it was moving very slowly, it was not until half an hour later that it came to a standstill.

When a train comes to a standstill in the middle of nowhere with darkness outside and snow falling and nobody knowing what has happened, and the guard hurrying by, as ignorant of what is wrong as all the passengers, there is a feeling that complete irrationality has taken over. The normal rules of life do not apply. Anything can happen. At any moment the train may start to plough forward again in its customary way, or it may remain standing where it is for hours, growing colder and colder. Realism prevents the mind from forecasting that this might last for days, since it is unlikely that in the commuter belt any train will be left stranded for long, but uneasiness makes itself apparent very soon. People know that they are at the mercy of forces over which they have no control. The amount of coughing increases. Newspapers rustle noisily. Feet scrape on the floor. Strangers begin to talk to one another.

A woman sitting opposite to Andrew tried to interest him in the fact that her bull-terrier, a dog that had once won a prize in a show, was now shut up in her house at home and would be working himself into a terrible state if she was late. Andrew expressed sympathy with the plight of the dog and meanwhile resigned himself to the fact that the train could not conceivably reach Maddingleigh on time. That meant that he would be late for his appointment with Henry Hewison. But perhaps the man would not try to reach the cottage if the blizzard was continuing. If he had any sense, Andrew thought, he would stay at home.

It astonished him to discover, when the train reached Maddingleigh only three quarters of an hour late, that it was not snowing. It was some time since he had tried peering out into the darkness to see what was happening and it was only when he emerged from the station that he realized that here it was a clear, starlit night. There was something terribly cold about the brilliance of the stars in the black sky, but underfoot the new snow was not very deep. The district had been spared the blizzard that had hit London. He walked to where he had left his car in the car-park, got into it and started the drive home.

He was half-way to Godlingham before he noticed anything amiss. When the strangeness had started he was not sure because his attention had been on his driving, on the long cone of light from his headlights cleaving the darkness of the road ahead of him. There was very little traffic on it that evening. But all at once he became aware that at a turning where there was a cluster of cottages, where at this time of the evening there would normally have been a number of lighted windows to be seen, there was only darkness. He could see the outlines of the cottages in the starlight, but not a glimpse of light in any window.

Driving up a slight rise from the top of which he ought to have been able to see the lights of Godlingham in the hollow before him, he could see nothing but a pool of the enveloping dark. His heart sank. A power failure. And on a bitter night like this. And in Peter's cottage there was no way of warming the place without electricity. He remembered Peter telling him that although the central heating was oil-fired, it depended on an electric pump for the hot water to circulate through the house. Yet cold might not be the most serious difficulty ahead of him, for it would take some hours for the warmth of the cottage to be completely dispersed. A more immediate problem would be light. It had not occurred to Andrew while he had been in the cottage to see if there was a stock of candles anywhere, and he did not relish the idea of blundering around with only the light of an electric torch that Peter had left in the kitchen, trying to cook his supper.

But of course he would not be able to cook any supper. The cooking stove would not work. So it would have to be bread and cheese.

The thought did not dismay him too much, as he had had an ample lunch and he knew that there was a portable gas heater stored in the garage, which he could wheel indoors and sit close to if the power cut continued. But he hated the thought of having to sit in the dark, unable to read, unable to watch television. There was a radio which worked on batteries, but except for listening to it, there would be nothing for him to do but twiddle his thumbs.

Approaching Godlingham, he saw that Simon Kemp's cottage, the Fidlers' and the Goodchilds' were all in darkness. So was the big house on the other side of the road. Driving his car into his garage, he saw the gas heater at the back of it and felt reassured by the knowledge that it was there in case he should really be reduced to needing it, then he locked the garage and took the path round the house to the front door. He had dug the path clear of snow the day before. Fragments of it that had been left behind were frozen hard and treacherous, but he walked carefully and was almost at the door when a bright light shone suddenly in his face.

His first impulse was to throw up a hand to shield his eyes from the glare. The light was switched off.

"I'm sorry," a woman's voice said. "I didn't mean to startle you. I've just been ringing your bell but there wasn't any answer, so I was going to leave when I saw your car drive up and I thought I'd wait."

The voice was familiar and so was the tall, slim figure in boots, trousers and a duffle-coat whom he could discern standing on his doorstep now that his eyes had recovered from the sudden flash of light. It was Ruth Kemp, he thought.

Then he realized that this woman was not as tall as the girl with whom he had walked on the downs, or as young.

"I'm Pauline Hewison," she went on. "I know you haven't anything but electricity in this cottage and heaven knows how long this cut will last. They've a genius for breaking down whenever the weather gets really bad. And the water's gone off too. I've been on to the electricity people about it by telephone and they say they've got trouble with one of the pumps. They wouldn't commit themselves as to how long it was likely to last. So I thought perhaps you might care to come over to me, because I've a good log fire that'll keep us warm and I've a gas camping-stove on which I can warm up something hot to eat. Will you come?"

"That's extraordinarily kind of you," Andrew said. "A log fire sounds delightful. But if you don't mind, I'll just go inside and deposit my brief-case and take a quick look round to see if there are any candles. If it's still going to be pitch-dark when I get back, I'd like to know where I can lay my hands on them."

"If there aren't any, I can supply you with some," she said. "I always keep a spare packet in the house in case of trouble like this. Take my torch, it'll help you look around."

"Thank you." He took the torch, switched it on and, as he felt for his key, pointed the beam at the keyhole.

It was only then that he realized that the door was not quite shut.

It disturbed him. He felt fairly sure that he had pulled it shut behind him when he left in the morning. It was something about which he was usually careful. Yet if he had done so the lock could not quite have clicked, for certainly the door was ajar now.

He pushed it open and stepped inside and led the way down the short passage to the sitting-room.

As he entered it he nearly fell over, tripping over something on the floor. For a moment he thought that he must

have left his slippers there and gave the object a light kick to
get it out of his way. But it hardly moved. It seemed to be
attached to something heavy that did not stir. Puzzled, he
pointed the beam of the torch downwards. What he had
kicked was a human hand and what it was attached to was
the body of Henry Hewison, who lay on a rug there with a
big dark stain on his chest.

Shocked into immobility and incredulous, Andrew stood
there, staring down. Then he saw the eyelids flicker and a
faint movement of the lips.

Henry Hewison was not dead and he was trying to tell
Andrew something.

CHAPTER 4

Andrew stooped quickly, trying to catch what was said, but now the lips were still.

He felt hopelessly incompetent to deal with the situation. Death was something that happened in hospitals. Other people, doctors, nurses, informed you that it had happened. But there was no nurse, no doctor present.

From behind him he heard Pauline Hewison say, "What is it? What's happened?"

"Perhaps you'd better come in," he said. He had a feeling that she was not a woman who would become hysterical. "Come in and shut the door."

She did as he said while he kept the beam of the torch directed onto the face of Henry Hewison.

She gave him a quick glance and put both of her gloved hands to her face. Her voice dropped to a whisper. "Is he dead?"

Andrew knelt down beside the still figure. "I'm not sure. I don't think so. He tried to say something."

He started feeling for the heart to see if he could feel even the faintest throb, but either it had stopped or else it was not in the place where he supposed hearts normally were. What else could you do, he wondered, to discover whether or not a person was dead?

Pauline Hewison was more practical than he was. Moving

cautiously across the dark room, she took a cushion from the sofa, brought it to where her brother-in-law lay, slid it gently under his head, then looked round and said, "Have you a blanket? I'm sure we shouldn't move him, but there must be a draught coming in under that door and I think we ought to cover him."

"I'll get one from upstairs," Andrew said, and went hurrying to the door.

"Wait," she said. "Can you find a candle? I'll phone Dr. Bell right away."

"Take the torch," Andrew said, holding it out to her and preparing to fumble his way up the stairs in the darkness.

As he did so he remembered the torch that Peter had left in the kitchen. As Pauline went to the telephone, Andrew went to the kitchen and felt for the torch on the shelf where he knew it was. His fingers found it and pressed the switch. Nothing happened. Though Peter had left him a torch, he had not thought of making sure that it had a live battery. Returning to the staircase, Andrew made his way up it.

Now that his eyes were accustomed to the darkness he could see a certain amount without much difficulty. The clear starlight that came through the windows at least lit up the shapes of furniture. He knew there were some folded blankets on the bed in the small bedroom where he had taken to working. He found one and took it downstairs.

Pauline was just putting down the telephone. Turning towards the man on the floor, she directed the beam of the torch onto him so that Andrew could arrange the blanket over him.

"Dr. Bell's out on a case," she said. "His wife's phoning his partner, but he lives in Croxley—that's about five miles away—so he'll take some time to get here with the roads in the state they're in. Shall we phone for an ambulance from Maddingleigh? It might get here as quickly as he will and in any case it's what he'll probably do himself."

"Yes—yes, I'm sure we should do that," Andrew said. "And then—I've had an idea. Mrs. Goodchild was a district nurse, wasn't she? She could be here in a minute or two and tell us if there's anything we can do."

"Hannah Goodchild? Oh no! An ambulance, yes, but Hannah Goodchild, no!" Pauline picked up the telephone and with fingers that suddenly seemed stiff with nervousness, dialled 999.

Andrew did not speak again until she had given her message, asking for an ambulance to be sent immediately, and had put the telephone down. Then he said, "All the same, I'm going to ask Mrs. Goodchild to come over. You may not be friends, but—"

"Friends!" Her voice, which had seemed calm enough until that moment, suddenly shot up wildly. "If that woman comes here, I shall leave!"

"I don't think you should, you know," Andrew said. "Not till the police have said you can."

"The police?" she said, still on the same shrill note.

"Of course," Andrew said. "You and I have found a man who's been shot, probably murdered. They'll want to know from both of us just what happened. We shouldn't be wasting time like this before calling them."

He heard her draw a deep breath, then saw her holding out the torch to him and her shadowy figure move away from the telephone.

"Of course." Her voice was low and quiet again.

"But I'm going to ring Mrs. Goodchild first," he said, and, picking up the book beside the telephone in which Peter had the numbers noted down that he used most often, found the Goodchilds' in it, dialled it, heard it ringing and waited.

Pauline sank down into a chair, crouching forward with her elbows on her knees and her face again held in both hands.

The Goodchilds' telephone was lifted.

"Goodchild speaking," a voice said.

"Mr. Goodchild, this is Basnett," Andrew said. "I believe you told me Mrs. Goodchild's a nurse."

"She was, yes," Goodchild said cautiously, as if this were something which perhaps he should not admit. "But she retired a long time ago."

"All the same, perhaps she can help now," Andrew said. "An appalling thing has happened. There's been an accident —no, that's nonsense. Why should I say an accident? I've just come home from London and found Hewison in my sitting-room, shot. On the floor. Dying, or perhaps dead. I'm not sure which. I'm not sure about anything. I'm not even sure if he was shot or stabbed or what. There's a lot of blood on his chest, that's all I know, and he's unconscious. And we've phoned for the doctor and an ambulance and I'm just going to phone the police, but I thought that in the meantime Mrs. Goodchild might come over and tell us if there's anything we can do."

"We?" Goodchild said sharply. "You aren't alone?"

"Mrs. Hewison is here with me," Andrew said. "We came in together and found him."

There was a long silence. It lasted for so long that Andrew did not know if Goodchild was still on the telephone or perhaps had wandered off to find his wife. But at least he had not rung off, for the dialling tone had not been resumed.

"Mr. Goodchild—" Andrew began.

"Yes, yes, we'll come, of course," Goodchild said. "I'll tell my wife, though in the circumstances—well, it can't be helped. We prefer to avoid contact—but I realize it's impor- tant—yes, very important. So we'll be over in a few minutes. But how did Hewison get into your sitting-room if you were in London?"

"I haven't the faintest idea," Andrew answered. "But Mrs. Goodchild will come?"

"Yes, yes, we'll come. At once."

The telephone was put down.

Andrew waited an instant, then dialled 999 and a moment later found himself speaking to a sergeant in the police station in Maddingleigh. Giving him his message, Andrew had to resist an impulse to let his voice rise, almost as Pauline's had, and become frenzied with impatience while the man made methodical notes of the facts that he was given and promised immediate action. He sounded alert and brisk enough, yet to Andrew it felt as if he were being deliberately slow and was determined to frustrate him.

Dropping into a chair, he suddenly became conscious of the fact that he was extremely tired. It had been a long day, apart from having to cope with murder at the end of it. Also, for the first time, he became aware that the room was very cold. He had not taken off his overcoat and now huddled it about him.

"What time was the power cut off?" he asked.

"About four o'clock, I think," Pauline answered. The shrillness had quite gone out of her voice. It sounded merely flat and empty. "Anyway, it was more or less dark already. For a time I just sat doing nothing, waiting for it to come on again, and then . . ." She paused, giving a deep sigh. "Then I couldn't bear it any longer. It began to feel just like that other time. The darkness, the cold . . . And I began to remember things I prefer not to think about. You know my story, I expect."

"Some of it, anyway," Andrew said.

"Yes, they'd have told you all about it, these people here. And probably you believe them. Well, it doesn't matter to me if you do. I came over to see you because suddenly I couldn't bear being alone. That great house and the utter emptiness of it and the darkness and the cold . . ." Her voice, which had sunk almost to a whisper, began to shake.

Hastily, because he did not want her to break down now of all times, Andrew said, "Isn't your daughter with you?"

"Ruth? She went to see Simon this afternoon. Simon Kemp. Do you know him?"

"I've met him."

"Do you know they're married?"

"Yes."

"So you'll also know they've broken up. But I think there's a chance they may make it up again."

"Would you like that?"

"I suppose so. I don't think it matters much. There'll be someone else, as there've been others before him, if it isn't Simon."

"But surely you aren't actually alone in the house. Haven't you servants?"

"I've a Portuguese couple who cook and look after it for me, but I let them go home for Christmas. They won't be back till next week. Usually I rather like being left alone. The way it hit me this evening was only because of the mixture of the snow and the power cut and the way it all repeated the awful thing that happened before. So I thought of asking you over, because I knew you wouldn't have any heating here and I thought perhaps you wouldn't have completely made up your mind about me. And now, of course, I wish to God I hadn't come. I might at least have kept out of all this."

"That reminds me," Andrew said, "did you notice if the front door was ajar when you got here?"

"No, I was just going to ring when you arrived. I didn't notice anything."

"If it had been ajar for some time, it explains why the room's so icy now. Normally, with the power not going off till four o'clock, it wouldn't have got cold so quickly."

"No." She gave an abrupt shiver, as if she had only just noticed the cold herself. "Don't you think it would be a good thing to see if you can find any candles? We ought not to keep that torch on any longer than we can help in case the battery gives out."

"Quite right. I'll see."

Andrew got to his feet again, though with a fearful sense of fatigue with which he was almost unable to struggle. Before starting towards the kitchen he directed the beam of the torch once more onto the figure on the floor, then with his weariness suddenly forgotten, he darted forward, kneeling down swiftly beside the man who he had thought was dead.

"Yes?" he said urgently. "Yes?"

For he had seen the lips move.

A faint sound came from them, a mumble that meant nothing, then one word was clear. ". . . Nesbit . . ." Then the mumble came again and then there was silence.

Andrew remained where he was for a moment, then he stood up.

"I think he's gone," he said.

Pauline stood up beside him. "What was that he said?"

What the impulse was that made him answer as he did Andrew did not understand. "I couldn't make it out," he said. "I'll see if I can find those candles now."

Leaving her alone again in the dark room, he went out to the kitchen to look for them.

He did not find any. When he returned to the sitting-room he found her standing where he had left her, gazing down fixedly at the shadowy figure on the floor.

"What was he doing here?" she asked. "Do you know?"

"I know more or less why he came," Andrew answered, "only not how he got in. But I expect we'll find that out in time."

"Why did he come, or is that private?" She moved away to a chair and sat down again.

Andrew sat down and switched off the torch. In the faint starlight that fell through the big window he could see the outline of her small head, dark against the pale cover of the chair. The chill in the room was creeping into his bones.

"He telephoned this morning and made an appointment to meet me here at five-thirty," he said. "He told me he'd received some rather curious information and he wanted to discuss it with someone who'd be dispassionate. Unluckily, my train was held up by the snow, so I arrived here very late."

"Information," she said. "Curious information. I think I can make a guess at what it was about."

"Have you seen him recently?"

"Oh no, we never see each other. All the same, I can guess—"

She was interrupted by the ringing of the doorbell.

Andrew switched on the torch again and went to open the door. The two Goodchilds stood aside, Godfrey Goodchild was holding a torch. Hannah was the first to step into the passage, with her husband close behind her.

"We came as quickly as we could," she said as she went into the sitting-room, then, looking down, exclaimed, "Oh, poor H.H.!"

But although she was a nurse and it was because of that that Andrew had summoned her, it was her husband who stooped over the recumbent figure, first shone the torch into the colourless face, then removed the spectacles that Henry Hewison wore, delicately lifted an eyelid and shone the torch full into the staring eye. He stayed there for a moment, then let the eyelid fall and straightened up.

"That's that," he said.

"Dead?" Andrew asked although he knew the answer.

"I'm afraid so," Goodchild replied. "So there's nothing Hannah and I can do. We may as well go home. You've phoned for the police, of course?"

There was a subtle change in his manner of which Andrew was immediately aware, though it took him a moment to recognize what it was. Then he realized that it was a note of decisiveness, almost of authority, in the normally vague and hesitant voice.

"Yes," Andrew said. "They should be here any time now."

"If they want us, they'll know where to find us. Come, Hannah, let's go."

"Mightn't it be a good thing for you to wait for them here?" Andrew said.

"Why?"

Andrew could not really think of a good reason why the Goodchilds should stay, he only felt that now that they were on the scene it would be best for them to remain.

"I don't suppose you saw Hewison arrive, did you?" he asked. "You didn't happen to notice when he got here?"

He thought Hannah Goodchild was going to answer, but with the strange new decisiveness in his tone her husband spoke first. "We don't spend much of our time looking out of our windows, observing the comings and goings of our neighbours. I certainly saw nothing."

Hannah was mute.

"I'm sorry we haven't been able to help," Goodchild went on, "but even if we'd got here sooner I don't think we'd have been able to do anything for the poor fellow. Now, as I said, if the police want us, they'll find us at home. They'd only find us in the way if we stayed here. There'll be quite a number of them, I expect. They'll soon overflow the place. They'll bring lights, of course. I wonder how much longer this damned power cut is going to last. Well, let us know if there's anything else we can do. Come, Hannah."

This time Andrew let them go. Returning to his chair and once more switching off the torch he held, he began to think about the Goodchilds' brief visit and to wonder what it was about it that worried him, apart from the fact that so far as he had been able to see, neither of them had even glanced at

Pauline Hewison. There was something else besides that that nagged at his mind, but he could not pin it down. Possibly, he thought, if he stopped thinking about it, it would become clear to him. Meanwhile, why should he not go out to the garage and bring in Peter's portable gas heater? It seemed a good idea. It might reduce the appalling cold in the room.

But then he reflected that the police would want as little as possible altered in the room until they arrived and that in any case some of the cold from which he was suffering came not only from the lack of heating in the house and the icy air that had seeped into it through the door that had stood ajar for he did not know how long, but from the dead body of Henry Hewison. It was its presence there that made Andrew's teeth inclined to chatter and made him wonder why he had not yet asked Pauline if she would care for some whisky. When he did so, she accepted it eagerly. They were both sitting there in the dark in silence and Andrew was feeling a faint warmth developing in him as he drank when the police arrived.

Goodchild had been right that in a short time the small house would seem to be overflowing. The man in charge introduced himself as Detective Superintendent Ashe, but there was a plain-clothes sergeant too, as well as one or two men in uniform, and there were men whose whole duty it seemed to be to erect floodlights so that the sitting-room and the garden outside sprang into almost alarming brightness. There was a photographer and a man who wanted, though he was not at first allowed to do it, to spray a grey powder everywhere, and there was a police surgeon who came from Maddingleigh, as well as the doctor from the village of Croxley, who arrived as a result of Pauline's call to Dr. Bell.

To be as little in the way of all these people as possible, Andrew withdrew with Pauline into the kitchen, where they were almost immediately followed by the superintendent, a stocky man of about forty-five with a square, blunt-featured face and slow speech with a good deal of his native Berkshire in it.

"I think we've met before, Mrs. Hewison," he said to Pauline as the three of them stood around the table in the centre of the small kitchen, where a light like the ones in the sitting-room had been placed. "I don't know if you remember me."

"I do indeed," she answered. "You were an inspector in those days."

"I was. And we had to ask you a great many questions then, as we'll have to do again tonight. But I'd like to leave that till later if you and Professor Basnett will just tell me a few things." He turned to Andrew. "It was you who discovered the body, I believe."

Andrew said that it was and in answer to a few questions told the superintendent of Henry Hewison's telephone call in the morning, of the appointment that had been made, of Andrew's lateness for it and of how he had encountered Mrs. Hewison on the doorstep, of the door being ajar and of how he had nearly fallen over the body in the sitting-room. But something made him keep to himself what he had heard Henry Hewison mumble the moment before he died. It was not that he wanted to keep it from the policeman, but he had a strong feeling that he did not want to mention it in front of Pauline Hewison.

She told the superintendent that she had come over to the cottage to invite Professor Basnett to her house because she knew that he had no means of heating here, or of cooking a meal, and that she had seen him drive up just as she reached the door.

"And if I may make a suggestion now, Mr. Ashe," she said, "I think if you would allow Professor Basnett to come home with me, we should be out of your way here and ourselves saved from freezing to death. As you know, it's only across the road, where you can reach us in a minute or two, and if you're afraid one or both of us might take the opportunity of vanishing into the night, you can send a man to keep an eye on us. He'll be welcome to a drink and at least will be warmer than here."

"I hardly think that'll be necessary," the superintendent replied. "But certainly go home, if that's what you'd prefer. And I'll be over presently when we've got things a bit sorted out here."

She looked at Andrew. "Will you come with me?"

"Thank you," he said. "I'll be very glad to."

Together they made their way through the men who crowded the passage, down the path where the freezing snow was already churned into slush by their coming and going, past the row of police cars and the ambulance in the main road and through the gates of Godlingham House.

It was only then that Andrew noticed that it had started snowing again. The starlight had gone and the snowflakes, visible in the beam of Pauline's torch, fell slanting in the wind out of the black cavern of the sky. He and Pauline walked side by side up the drive. As he saw how she walked with a long, confident stride over the slippery ground, he was reminded of how her daughter had walked on the downs. She took him to the portico of the house, unlocked the door and let him in.

The hall was in darkness, but as the light from her torch moved across it he had a glimpse of panelled walls, a high ceiling, fine doorways and a graceful staircase. Then she opened one of the doors and firelight greeted them. It seemed very bright after the darkness outside, though the heap of logs in the grate was only smouldering. But enough of a glow came from it to show a big room, panelled like the hall, with three tall windows covered by brocade curtains, a high ceiling with a finely moulded cornice and a great crystal chandelier hanging from the centre of it, a chandelier from which of course no light came. The furniture was stiff-looking and formal, but elegant. The room felt most agreeably warm after the cold outside.

Pauline walked to the fireplace, stirred up the fire with a poker and tossed some more logs onto it from a copper scuttle that stood by the side of the hearth.

As flames went leaping up the chimney, she said, "I'll get a lamp. Take your coat off and come and sit down and get warm. I'll get drinks in a minute."

She went out.

Andrew did as she said, dropping his coat on to a chair by the door, then sitting down as close as he could to the blaze. He could see the room clearly now and thought that in spite of the warm firelight, which threw dancing shadows over the floor and walls, and although it had a kind of stately beauty, there was something chillingly impersonal about it, almost as if nobody lived there.

He was left to himself for several minutes, then Pauline returned, carrying an old-fashioned oil-lamp.

"I'm sorry I was so long," she said, "but this was stuck away at the back of a cupboard. Luckily there's a little oil left in it. And if it gives out, as I told you, I've lots of candles." She lit the lamp, which added its soft light to that of the leaping fire. "It's really rather nice, isn't it? Not too good if one wanted to read or write, of course, but somehow kind to one when one only wants to sit and talk."

She had taken off her duffle-coat and her boots and was wearing a high-necked, sleek white sweater with her trousers, and flat-heeled, embroidered slippers.

"That poor man outside," she went on, "why shouldn't they let him come in and sit by the fire with us?"

"You think he's there, do you, keeping an eye on us?" Andrew said.

"Of course. I've been through this before, remember. And

I'm the perfect suspect, don't you think? I'm almost surprised they haven't arrested me already."

"You don't mean that," he said. "They've nothing against you."

"Oh, haven't they! You've told them Henry wanted to see you to discuss some information he'd got and that you arrived and found me on your doorstep with the door open. So it's possible I'd just come out of the house, isn't it, after shooting Henry, and that you caught me just before I could get away? And the information he'd got, or thought he'd got, was possibly something to do with Charles's murder. He was always certain I did it, you know, and he's always done his best to make everyone else believe it."

"So your daughter told me, but I understood you'd a perfect alibi."

"A little thing like an alibi meant nothing to Henry. Once he'd made up his mind about anything, there you were, there was no changing it. And he wanted me to be guilty because he'd have got all Charles's money. And what Henry wanted he thought he could have. Now I'll get those drinks. Whisky again?"

"Please."

She went out, moving soft-footedly in her slippers across the polished floor.

When she came back she gave Andrew his drink, then sat down facing him across the hearth. He saw now that she was wearing a good deal of make-up and thought that she had touched it up while she had been out of the room, and that possibly it was that, in the gentle light, that made her look so young. Too young to be the mother of the girl whom he had met on the downs.

"If Hewison didn't believe in your alibi," he said, "why did he think the Fidlers gave you one?"

She laughed. Andrew thought that she wanted it to sound light, but there was a bitter note in it.

"He was capable of thinking there was something between Jack and me," she said. "But there was the awkward fact, from his point of view, that Amabel backed Jack up. And the truth is, I always had a far closer relationship with her than I ever did with him. I always found him a bullying sort of person, as well as a bit of a bore. But Amabel I liked quite well." It sounded tolerant rather than warm.

"I was with them on Christmas Day," Andrew said. "They spoke of you as if you avoid them nowadays. They seemed to regret it."

"But isn't it the best thing I can do for them? And for myself, I expect you think. If we seem to be too close friends people might really start wondering if they faked that alibi just to oblige me. And that would be almost as bad for them as for me, because it would make them accessories after the fact." She drank some whisky, then held her glass up so that she could look through it at the lamp, and without turning towards him said, "Tell me, do you think I'm a murderess?"

He thought it best to laugh, hoping that it sounded more convincing than it had when she had laughed. "May I reserve judgement?"

As he said it he thought suddenly of how Peter had told him that there was something about the woman which had always made him feel that she was capable of murder. But here he sat, enjoying her hospitality and not wanting to think ill of her.

"If the police suspect you of what happened today," he said, "they'll have to explain how you knew my train was going to be late, because if I'd been in time to keep my appointment with Hewison I'd have been there with him, or anyway waiting for him, when you went over to the house."

"Why, then I'd have shot you both," she answered. "That's simple. They'll make nothing of that."

"Then why didn't you shoot me when I caught you on the

doorstep? It was dark. No one would have seen what happened. You could have done it and got away."

"Now why didn't I think of doing that?" She turned to look at him, smiling a malicious little smile. "And what did I do with the gun? Perhaps I've got it on me now."

"Dressed as you are," he said, "I've a suspicion it might show."

"Well, perhaps I disposed of it while I was getting the lamp, or our drinks. They didn't search me."

"I believe they never found the gun that killed your husband, did they?" Andrew said.

She dropped her bantering tone. "No. It was one of the things that helped me. And it wasn't for want of looking for it. They turned the place upside-down."

"And what's your own belief about what happened?"

For an instant she looked startled, almost as if no one else had ever asked her that question before. Then she said, "I know it sounds too convenient, but I've always thought it was just some burglar, one of those horrible adolescents perhaps that one reads about—"

She broke off as they heard the front door opened and closed, then quick steps crossing the hall. Ruth Kemp came into the room.

She was dressed as she had been when Andrew had met her on the downs in a duffle-coat, trousers and boots, with a knitted cap on her head on which he saw the gleam of fresh snowflakes. She looked so like her mother, so near her in age, that he would have assumed that they were sisters if he had not known their relationship. Ruth looked flushed and breathless.

"What's happened?" she demanded. "What are all those police doing there? Why is there a man at the gate who wouldn't let me come in till I told him who I was? Why is there an ambulance there?" It was only then that she appeared to notice Andrew's presence. "And what's Professor

Basnett doing here? Has Peter come back? Is it something to do with him? Has something awful happened?"

"Yes!" Pauline's tone was like a sudden sharp slap on the girl's face, meant to quieten her instantly. "But it's nothing to do with Peter. To the best of my knowledge he's in Paris. Someone had the remarkably good idea of shooting your uncle Henry. Now if you'll calm down and go and take those boots off before the snow on them starts melting, I'll tell you just what happened."

Ruth gave her a stunned look, which her mother met with one so imperative that the girl seemed to shrink from it, then turned and almost ran out of the room.

"You don't pretend to any grief," Andrew remarked.

"Grief!" Pauline said contemptuously.

"Relief—is that what you're feeling?"

"It may be. I haven't thought about it yet. For one thing, I don't know what I'm in for, do I?"

"You and your daughter are very alike."

"So everyone says."

"What sort of man was Hockley?"

"What sort of man was—*who?*" She gave him a stare of surprise.

"Hockley. Wasn't that your first husband's name? Ruth told me it was her real name. She doesn't seem to like being called Kemp or Hewison."

"Oh, I see." She gave a sardonic laugh. "There was never any man called Hockley. That happened to be simply my own name. Ruth is illegitimate. And she's rather proud of the fact. She almost revels in it. I hope it doesn't shock you."

"One would get worn out with shock these days if one let a thing like that disturb one," Andrew said. "Did she ever know her father?"

"No, and nor did I, to speak of. He was a very brief encounter. But at least I know who he was, if that reassures you about my character. He was in the Army, very young, very handsome, very stupid and horribly scared about his career when he realized what had happened." The door opened and Ruth came in again, looking less like her mother with her dark hair combed out in soft curls over her shoulders and wearing a frilly blue blouse with her trousers. "Well, Ruth, get yourself a drink and come and sit down and I'll tell you the worst. Only the worst is still to happen, I suppose, as far as I'm concerned. But that's self-centred. Never mind. I've never pretended to be anything else. Where have you been?"

"With Simon. Don't worry about that. What's happened?"

Pauline told her. She told her exactly what she and Andrew had told Superintendent Ashe. Andrew did not try to add anything to it. Watching her, he wondered if he was more attracted or repelled by her. He did not know if the callousness of her tone, the almost mocking way in which she spoke of the death of her brother-in-law, made him feel more revulsion or pity. In itself it shocked him, but there was the possibility that it was only a tone that she had chosen in self-defence because, as she had said, she had been through this before and now in reality was deeply frightened.

And after all, she had cause to be. As she herself had pointed out in her ironic way, the door had been open when he had arrived at the cottage and she could as easily just have come out of it as been waiting to be let in. She could have brought the gun away in the pocket of her coat and hidden it somewhere in the house while she had been fetching the lamp or the drinks. And if she had known that Henry Hewison had some curious information which he wanted to discuss with Andrew, and if she had reason to suspect that it was something to do with the murder of her husband, she could have had a motive for the murder.

Ruth kept her gaze on her mother's face all the time that she was talking. When she finished, the girl said nothing for a moment, then she gave her slender body a slight shake, like a dog shaking water off its coat, swallowed some of her drink and said, "Well, that's that. There's nothing we can do about it for the present. What are we doing about supper?"

Andrew doubted if she was really as composed as she meant to sound.

"I'll warm up something presently," Pauline answered. "Where did you leave Simon, if you've been with him?"

"In the Mitre, in Croxley," Ruth said. "I went to see him this afternoon with an idea we might sort something out and perhaps pick up the pieces somehow, and we talked for a bit and I thought we were getting somewhere. We were quite friendly, anyway. And then we started quarrelling, as we always used to, so I came away."

"In your car?"

"Yes."

"And you went in your car?"

"Yes."

"Then how will he get home?"

"He'll have to walk."

"That sounds a splendid way of trying to mend your marriage."

Ruth gave a nervous giggle. "I dare say I shouldn't have done it if I hadn't seen it was past mending."

The woman and the girl stared at one another with the same intensity on both their faces. Andrew recognized some strong antagonism in the look, but thought that perhaps neither of them was aware of how clearly it showed.

"So that's why you really came down for Christmas," Pauline said. "To see Simon and try to get him away."

"Well, partly," Ruth answered.

"And I thought you might have come because just for once you didn't want me to be alone at Christmas."

"Well, that too, of course."

"There's no 'of course' about it!" Pauline sprang to her

feet, suddenly taut with anger. "But Simon won't move, you found that out, did you? You can't always have everything your own way. That's what you quarrelled about in the Mitre, wasn't it? And it's why you left him to walk home through the snow."

Ruth shrugged her shoulders. "I'm sorry I did that now. It was rather mean of me. But why should he think I'd settle down to live here when I'd have nothing on earth to do? When we got married I thought he was going to look for a job in London."

"We aren't far from London. You could have kept your job on and gone up to it by train. Lots of people do that. But you didn't want to settle down so close to me, did you?"

"Mother," Ruth said softly, "we've got company."

Pauline started, catching her breath and smothering what she had been about to say. She turned to Andrew with a smile.

"I'm sorry," she said. "We shouldn't inflict our family problems on you, but I'm terribly on edge. I don't know what I'm saying. Ruth and I often fall out about nothing. We've got the same sort of tempers. And the thought of that poor man trudging home through the snow—"

"It wasn't snowing when I left him," Ruth interrupted, "and a strong man like him, all muscle, shouldn't mind it."

"Of course, now that Henry's dead," her mother said, "Simon may have second thoughts about staying on here."

"As I understood what Mr. Hewison told me," Andrew said, "the school was going to close down soon anyway from lack of money."

"So I've heard," Ruth answered. "All the staff know it and are looking for other jobs. And that's partly why I thought I might be able to persuade Simon to leave. But he wouldn't listen to me." She stood up. "I'll get the supper. What's it to be? The remains of yesterday's stew?"

"I'll see to it," Pauline said and went out quickly, afraid,

Andrew thought, that if she remained she might let her anger with her daughter show too plainly.

The so-called stew turned out to be an excellent goulash which had not suffered at all by being warmed up on the gas camping-stove. They ate at a table in the big drawing-room, which appeared to be the only room in which a fire had been lit. Andrew was becoming so accustomed to the dim light from the oil-lamp that it was coming to seem almost a normal means of illumination and that there would be nothing surprising about it, living here in the country, if the electric power should never be restored.

There was something almost nostalgically pleasant about it. He had spent his childhood in a village in Hampshire where electricity had not yet been thought of and where oil-lamps in the sitting-room and going to bed by the light of a single candle and cooking on a great coal range had all been taken for granted. No one had ever dreamt that improvements on these arrangements might ever be made.

The meal was almost silent. Andrew made no attempt to talk and the mother and daughter had taken to avoiding looking at one another. He sensed that Pauline was listening apprehensively for something to happen and he assumed that this was the arrival of the police, but the meal was finished and cleared away, though not washed up, as the water as well as the electricity was still cut off, before they arrived.

It was only Superintendent Ashe and the sergeant who came then. Ruth went to the door when they rang and brought them into the drawing-room, where the superintendent expressed pleasure at the sight of a fire and held out his hands to it, rubbing them together and saying that it was a treat to see a real log fire these days and there was a lot to be said for old-fashioned ways.

"That house of yours is an icebox, Professor," he said to

Andrew, "and we've had to have doors standing open, which hasn't helped. And there's no telling how long this cut will last. I've been on to the electricity people and they say some cable was brought down by the wind and they don't know how long it's going to take to mend it." He turned to Pauline. "Two days it lasted that other time, wasn't it, Mrs. Hewison?"

She nodded distantly.

"I remember it well," he said. "And it's snowing hard again now and there's no telling how long that'll go on either. The road may be blocked by morning. There's a nasty patch between here and Maddingleigh where it always gets blown into drifts. Well now, if you don't mind, I'd like to have a short talk with each of you separately. Perhaps there's another room we could use."

Pauline replied that they could use the dining-room, though no fire had been lit there. Leading the way out, she left Andrew and her daughter facing one another on either side of the fire.

Ruth leant back in her chair and closed her eyes and sat there quite motionless, which Andrew thought was less because she was as tired as she seemed to want to make out than because she wanted to shut herself off from him into her own brooding thoughts. By the time that Pauline returned, the fire had burnt low and, as Ruth did not attend to it, Andrew had taken it on himself to add some logs to it and stir it up. The flames were leaping up again when Pauline came in at last, followed by the sergeant, who asked Andrew if he would be so good as to come to the other room for a few minutes.

Andrew went with him across the dark hall into another high-panelled room, which was lit only by four candles. They were in two silver candlesticks that stood on a long mahogany table, where the superintendent sat with some papers spread before him, the faint light making his square, blunt face look a shadowy map of projections and hollows. The room felt very cold after the comfort of the drawing-room.

"Come and sit down, Professor," Ashe said, indicating a chair near him. "I won't keep you long. I just want to go over what you told me before and make sure I've got it straight."

He then went over the questions that he had asked Andrew in the cottage and Andrew answered them as before. As he concluded, Ashe nodded thoughtfully.

"Yes, and the puzzling thing, as I see it at the moment, is how Mr. Hewison got into your cottage. You're sure you closed the door properly when you left in the morning?"

"As sure as one can be about a thing like that," Andrew said. "I certainly intended to pull it shut behind me, but I suppose the lock may be faulty and it may have sprung open of itself."

"We've tested it," Ashe said, "and there doesn't seem to be anything wrong with it."

"Then it looks as if someone let him in, doesn't it?"

"Can you suggest who might have done that? Has anyone besides yourself got a key?"

"So far as I know, only Mrs. Nesbit, who comes in once a week to clean for me. But that reminds me . . ."

"Yes?" Ashe said as Andrew paused.

"Something I should tell you," he said, "though I don't know if it's of any significance. I told you Mr. Hewison wasn't actually dead when I found him, didn't I? Well, just before he died he spoke. He seemed to be trying to tell me something and he mumbled several words, but I only caught one of them and I can't really swear I got it right. But what I think he said was 'Nesbit.' "

"Just 'Nesbit'?"

"Yes."

Ashe rubbed a thick finger down one side of his jaw. "He may have been trying to tell you it was Mrs. Nesbit who let him in. Last words aren't always important. They can be about very trivial things. Have you any idea what she might have been doing in the house this afternoon?"

Andrew shook his head. "And I don't know how Mr. Hewison arrived at the cottage. It's a longish walk from the school, specially in weather like this, but there was no car outside."

"I can tell you that," Ashe said. "He was given a lift by Mr. Fidler. Soon after you and Mrs. Hewison came over here Mr. Fidler came round to us to find out what was going on, and he told us he'd overtaken Mr. Hewison on the road, evidently intending to come here on foot, and had picked him up and driven him to your gate. Although it's holidays up at the school, Mr. Fidler had been there, doing some sorting out of his things. He told us Mr. Hewison suffered from cataract and didn't like to drive in the dark, but he was an active man, so the walk wouldn't have been too much for him even if he hadn't got a lift. Still, there's something peculiar about it, specially for a man with bad eyesight. Tell me—" He hesitated. "Tell me, when you arrived, did you find a torch anywhere in the house?"

"There was one in the kitchen, where my nephew left it," Andrew answered. "But it doesn't work. The battery's dead."

"Just so. And you didn't see any other?"

"No."

"Nor did we. And doesn't it seem strange to you that a man should set out for a long walk in the dark, a man, as I said, with bad eyesight, without a torch?"

"I suppose it does. But it was a bright starlit evening when he started out."

"And you think he might have trusted to that lasting instead of its coming on to snow again, as it has?"

"It's possible, isn't it? Apart from that," Andrew went on, thinking of the flat tonic and the mislaid brandy, "I think he was an absent-minded sort of man who might simply not have thought about a thing like a torch if he didn't happen to need one at the moment. Has Mr. Fidler told you if he was using a torch when he overtook him?"

"He says he doesn't remember. He didn't notice it particularly."

"So perhaps he hadn't one. May I ask you why it matters?"

Ashe took a little while to reply, as if he were not sure if he meant to answer the question, then he observed, "Mrs. Hewison had a torch. She had it when you found her on your doorstep, didn't she?"

"Yes, she shone it in my face . . . Oh, I see!" Andrew wondered why he had not understood from the beginning to what this line of questioning was leading, particularly in view of what Pauline had said to him earlier about the fact that the police were certain to suspect her. "You think she'd been into the house and was just coming away, not arriving, when I caught her there, and that the torch was one she'd picked up in the house after Mr. Hewison dropped it when she shot him."

"That's one of the possibilities we've got to consider," Ashe replied.

"Are there others?"

"Oh yes. But I wouldn't like to commit myself to any theory just yet. It's a fact, all the same, that for Mrs. Hewison to have popped across the road from this house without a torch in that bright starlight you mentioned seems to me less unlikely than that Mr. Hewison should have set out without one on that long walk from the school."

"But why should she have taken his away with her, if she'd just committed a murder?" Andrew asked. "If she'd used it, it might have been seen by someone, as in fact I saw it, and drawn attention to her having been there."

"True. But people sometimes make worse mistakes than that when they've just committed a murder. Even professionals do it, not only amateurs. I think we can be sure this was an amateur job. She may have picked it up to see just what she'd done to him, or something like that, then carried it out without thinking. Well, thank you for your help. I think that's all I need to ask you at present."

Andrew got up and went out. The sergeant followed him, presumably to fetch Ruth to the dining-room to be questioned in her turn. But as he and Andrew were making their way across the dark hall the doorbell rang and the sergeant, instead of going on to the drawing-room, went to the front door and opened it.

Two figures were standing in the shelter of the portico. One carried a torch and pointed it at the sergeant, then swept its beam around the hall, stopping suddenly as it lighted on Andrew. The world outside was full of almost invisible movement as snowflakes came drifting down on to the whitely gleaming ground.

"May we come in?" a man's voice asked.

As he said it the drawing-room door opened and Pauline came out. In the dim light that came through the open door it was possible to recognize Jack and Amabel Fidler, both in anoraks with their hoods up, trousers and boots.

"Oh, it's you," Pauline said in a tone of hostile arrogance. "What do you want?"

"We've heard what's happened," Amabel said. "Jack went over when he saw all the police cars—"

"And we were told you'd walked in on it," her husband interrupted in his usual way, "and we thought we might be able to help somehow."

"Help?" Pauline said. She made the word sound immensely scathing. "What do you suppose you can do for me this time?"

"Oh, don't talk like that, Pauline," Amabel began again. "We just thought—"

"We thought you might be glad to know you've got friends

who'll stand by you in any trouble," her husband said.
"We're sorry—terribly sorry—about what's happened."

"So am I, but our reasons might be different," Pauline
said.

"Shall we come in?" Amabel asked.

"I'd sooner you didn't," Pauline replied coldly. "I don't
feel like a cosy chat about another murder. I can understand
you don't want me to be suspected. Of course you don't. But
I don't see what you can do about it. And the police are here
and so are Ruth and Professor Basnett. That's enough company for the present."

"I was just going to say," Andrew said, "that I think I ought
to go home. Thank you very much for that delicious dinner,
a remarkable achievement in the circumstances, and for
keeping me warm, but I mustn't impose on you any longer. I
imagine the police will allow me back into my own home
now."

"If you don't mind, sir," the sergeant said, "we were going
to ask you if you could make arrangements to sleep somewhere else tonight. We shan't be finished in there for some
time yet and it's so small, we shan't be able to keep out of
your way. You'll have a very disturbed time. If you like we'll
get you a room in the Green Dragon and one of our cars will
drive you there."

Courteously as it was put, it was an order.

But before Andrew could agree to it, Amabel said, "Oh,
don't go there. Come and spend the night with us. Of course
we haven't any heating as we're all electric like you, but
we've a gas radiator and can boil up some water for a hot-
water bottle for you and manage breakfast for you in the
morning. Do please come."

"But I really can't trouble you like that," Andrew was
beginning when Fidler broke in once more, "No trouble, no
trouble at all. Glad to have you. Only want to be good
neighbours. I wish Pauline would understand that, but some

day perhaps she will. Will you come with us now, Professor?"

Andrew thanked the Fidlers, thanked Pauline once more, said goodbye to her, put on his overcoat and went out with the Fidlers into the steadily falling snow and icy darkness.

As they went down the drive, where walking had become very difficult, each of the Fidlers took one of Andrew's arms and spoke encouragingly to him as they made their way to the gate, as if they were afraid that he might fall down or find the short walk to their house too much for him, if they did not support him. It made him feel very old, or at least it made him admit to himself, which he very often did not, because he did not always feel it, that seventy was an advanced age which undoubtedly seemed very old to this relatively young couple.

They escorted him first to his cottage, where he was able to pick up pyjamas, a dressing-gown, a tooth-brush and a razor, then on to their home, where they took his coat from him and placed him in a chair close to the gas radiator, which they had left burning in their sitting-room while they had been out. Then Amabel insisted on boiling up some water, which she drew from the tank since there was still no water in the main tap, for a hot-water bottle for his bed, even though he protested that this was a luxury to which he never treated himself. But later, when he went to bed, he was glad of it. It seemed to relieve the extreme fatigue which overwhelmed him once more as soon as he relaxed. He drifted off to sleep almost immediately.

But just before he sank into unconsciousness an odd thought came to him. He seemed to be back in Peter's cottage, watching as Godfrey Goodchild stooped over the body of Henry Hewison, delicately lifted an eyelid, shone a torch straight into the eye, then straightened up and said, "That's that." Said it with absolute certainty. Yet what a strange thing it was for him to have done. Andrew would never have thought of it himself. If it had occurred to him to look into the dead man's eye, he would not have known what it might tell him.

In that moment he became convinced that whatever Godfrey Goodchild might be now, he had at one time in his life been a doctor. Yet he did not want anyone to know it. It really was very odd. Then sleep came and put an end to Andrew's cogitation.

CHAPTER 5

When Andrew awoke, the room was dark and it took him a little while to remember where he was, and why, when he had done that, he was there. But as recollection of the evening before came back he put out a hand to where, before going to sleep, he had noticed a reading-lamp on a table by the bed, found the switch and pressed it, hoping that the electric power had been restored during the night. But nothing happened. However, the candle by the light of which he had come to bed was on the table. He found the matchbox beside it, lit the candle and looked at his watch. It was seven o'clock, his usual time for waking.

He was warm and comfortable in bed, but his arms, reaching out from under the bedclothes to the candle, felt most unpleasantly cold. Shrinking back hurriedly into the cocoon of blankets, he began to wonder what he ought to do about getting up. He supposed that the Fidlers would call him when they themselves got up and started to do something about preparing breakfast, but they had not told him last night when they normally did this.

There was no sound yet of movement in the house and he soon began to feel restless. It was his habit to get up soon after seven and the older he got the more habit dominated his life. Trying to lie still with the bedclothes swathing as much of his head as possible, so that little but his nose pro-

jected into the icy room, he found himself half-whispering
the rhyme that had haunted him for the last few days.

> "There was a pig went out to dig . . .
> There was a cow went out to plough . . ."

With his eyes on the small flame of the candle, he remembered that there were no candles in Peter's cottage, and that
meant that if this power-cut continued, he would have to
plough his way into the village to buy some. Not an attractive thought, as he still had no boots. But perhaps he could
beg some candles from the Fidlers, or from Pauline
Hewison. She had offered him some the evening before,
though in his somewhat sudden departure from her house
with the Fidlers the matter had been forgotten. But the
truth was that he was not sure that he wanted to see her
again. He did not know what he made of the events of the
previous evening, but he knew that the woman herself
made him feel strangely uneasy. He did not go quite so far as
suspecting her of the murder of her brother-in-law, yet he
could not help feeling that there was a certain hardness, a
lack of innocence, about her whole personality, which made
him feel that she might be capable of anything. And he did
not want to be drawn into friendship with a murderess.

While he was thinking about this the door opened and
Amabel Fidler came in, carrying a tray.

"Here's some tea," she said. "I boiled up some snow for
the water and I think it's all right, and here's a jug of hot
water if you want to shave. I didn't want to risk using up the
water in the tank in case it doesn't start running again for
some time."

"Tea sounds wonderful," Andrew said. "You're very good
to me."

"That's all right," she said. "I'll have breakfast ready in
about half an hour."

She went out and Andrew reached out an arm from under the bedclothes to pour out a cup of tea.

Drinking it meant sitting up in the cold, but still, it was cheering. Faint daylight was appearing at the window. When he had drunk two cups he began to face the ordeal of getting up and hurriedly huddling himself into his clothes. But as he did so he began to wonder if he could ask Amabel for a small piece of cheese before his breakfast. He was so used to having one, so sure that a little protein was necessary to him to set him up for the day, that the thought of going without it made him feel almost like being deprived of a drug. But if he asked for it Amabel might think it an eccentric taste and though he was ready to admit to himself that he had a number of small eccentricities of a harmless kind, he dreaded the thought that anyone else should know about them. So he would survive without cheese, he decided.

As it turned out, he had no need to fear having to start the day without protein. When he came downstairs to breakfast, Amabel provided him with bacon and two fried eggs. She apologized for the fact that there was no toast but only plain bread to go with the butter and marmalade, but the toaster, she said, would not work, and though she had been able to fry the bacon and eggs on her gas ring, she could not make toast over the flame. Daylight had come and the room with its pale furniture and bright curtains and with the radiator alight was very pleasant. Outside, the world was still and white, beginning to glisten in the brightening sunshine.

Jack Fidler did not eat bacon and eggs but only had coffee and an apple.

"Got to watch my weight," he said. "Amabel's cooking makes it a fearful trial of strength to keep it down. Just those few days over Christmas I put on four pounds. All the same, now and then one's got to let oneself go and enjoy oneself, hasn't one? Not that I ought to be talking of our enjoying ourselves after what happened last night. You know, I'm terribly sorry for Pauline. I don't want you to get a wrong idea about her because of the way she talked to us last night. She knows we're her friends and she only puts up that sort of show because she thinks people won't believe in that alibi we gave her when her husband was killed if we're on too close terms."

"She said something of the sort to me herself yesterday," Andrew said.

"She's making a mistake, of course." The apple crunched in Fidler's teeth as he munched it. "But she's a stubborn woman. We've given up trying to get her to change her mind about keeping up a normal relationship with us. But last night we felt we had to go and see her. We didn't know you'd be with her, or Ruth either. We thought she'd gone back to London. So we thought Pauline would be all alone and needing someone to talk to, because it looks as if the police may really have got it in for her this time. A rotten business. She wouldn't hurt a fly."

Andrew could imagine Pauline hurting any number of flies if she had a suitable weapon to use against them, but there was no need to say so.

"Something I can't understand is why she didn't move away after her husband's death," he said. "She doesn't seem to have any friends here."

"Well, I wouldn't be altogether surprised if she does go now," Fidler remarked.

"Now that her brother-in-law is dead?"

Fidler nodded. "Of course, I don't actually know . . . I just had a feeling sometimes that H.H. had some sort of power over her. I may be quite wrong. As I say, it's just a feeling."

"What will happen to the school now that he's dead?" Andrew asked. "Will it close down right away?"

"Oh, I don't think so."

"But he told me he was expecting to have to close it down

soon for financial reasons. Does his being dead make any difference to that?"

Fidler hesitated. The apple crunched. "I know I oughtn't to be saying this kind of thing," he said, "but the fact is, I think that with H.H. out of the way, Pauline might be persuaded to put some money into it. It's actually run by a trust, you know, and with someone else in charge she might—but I'm only guessing—she might come to the rescue."

"If it closes, will you and your wife have to move away?"

"I suppose so, if I can get a job anywhere else. Unemployment is pretty acute these days in the teaching profession, as I'm sure you know. Anyway, it's unlikely I'd ever find anything that suits me as well as the job I've got at Newsome's. The place has an atmosphere. Perhaps not all that poor old H.H. believed, but still, it's distinctive. So I hope we can stay on."

"Mrs. Hewison really hated her brother-in-law, did she?" Andrew said.

The Fidlers looked at one another and for a moment neither answered. Then Amabel, sounding gentle yet somehow implacable, and with her straight strong brows drawn together, said, "I don't think we ought to go on talking like this. We'll say something we regret."

Her husband nodded. "But since the matter's come up, I think I might as well say that H.H. really hated Pauline. He was sure she'd killed his brother. He wasn't logical about it. He wasn't a logical sort of man. He just had intense beliefs, and that was one of them."

"But in that case, what were his feelings about you?" Andrew asked. "Because if he believed Mrs. Hewison killed her husband he can't have believed in the alibi you gave her. Yet here you are, years later, still teaching in his school and apparently on reasonably good terms with him, since I understand he accepted a lift from you yesterday to go to my cottage."

"That's right," Fidler agreed. "But he didn't like me. He couldn't have got rid of me without a fearful fuss. You can't sack a man simply because he's told the police what they've accepted as the truth. If he'd tried to do anything of the sort I think the N.U.T. would have taken up my case."

Andrew had finished his bacon and eggs with enjoyment and was eating bread and marmalade. "What mood was he in when you picked him up yesterday evening?" he asked.

"Pretty taciturn," Fidler said, "but that was nothing unusual. As I said, he didn't like me. He wouldn't have gone out of his way to make conversation, just out of friendliness. But he thanked me quite pleasantly when I put him down at your gate."

"I believe you've told the police you aren't sure whether or not he had a torch with him."

"No, I can't remember seeing one, but he may have had one in his pocket. When my headlights picked him up on the road I didn't notice one, but he might have switched it off when I pulled up beside him. I didn't wait to see what he did when he started up the path to your door. I simply backed the car and drove into the garage here. So perhaps he had a torch that he switched on then, but I really don't know."

"Oh, look!" Amabel suddenly exclaimed. She was standing by the window, looking out at the gleaming white lawn. "Here's Simon with a bucket of something. Water, I do believe. Wait a minute."

She went quickly out of the room and Andrew heard her open the front door and greet Simon Kemp.

After a moment she brought him into the sitting-room.

"Simon's brought us a bucketful of water from his well," she said. "Isn't that kind?"

"Don't drink it," Kemp said. If he had walked home from Croxley the evening before, he looked none the worse for it. His ruddy cheeks had a healthy glow and his amiable blue eyes were bright. There were no signs about him that he had suffered from the cold. "I haven't used that old well in the garden since I moved into the cottage, so God knows what the water's like, but I thought you might find it useful for washing-up and flushing the loo and so on. And if you want some more I can easily draw it up for you. Luckily, it hasn't frozen."

"That's very thoughtful of you, Simon," Amabel said. "I've been making tea and coffee with melted snow, but getting enough of it for other purposes felt a bit beyond me. I thought I'd just let everything pile up till the power and the water come on again, but now I can do some clearing-up. All the same, this cut can't last much longer, d'you think?"

"God knows," Kemp said. "You'd think if it was just a case of some lines coming down, they'd have got it repaired by now, but there's nothing we can do about it but put up with it. To tell the truth, I'm rather enjoying it. I've got a good fire going in that great old fireplace of mine and it looks marvellous and I'm pretty comfortable."

"Well, have some coffee," Amabel suggested.

Kemp accepted a cup and sat down at the table. "About what happened last night . . ." he began, then stopped, looking embarrassed.

Fidler spoke hurriedly. "None of us knows anything about it, Simon. We've been going round and round it with Professor Basnett, who spent the night with us because the police have taken over his house, and we've been getting nowhere. I suggest we leave it to the police. Have they been to see you?"

"Not yet," Simon said. "Or if they came yesterday, it was while I was out. Of course I saw the police cars in the road and I chatted to one of the constables and he told me what had happened, but they haven't been round to question me yet. Ruth came in, in the afternoon and we did a lot of talking. I wish she hadn't. We don't get anywhere and it only unsettles us. But we drove off to the pub in Croxley for a drink and then we had a real row and she drove off and I had to walk home. Of course I cursed her because she meant me to, but as a matter of fact, I enjoyed it. Wonderful stuff, snow. We don't get enough of it in this country. I'm going to Switzerland next week for some skiing. I suggested to Ruth she might go with me, but she wouldn't hear of it. By the way . . ."

"Yes?" Amabel said.

"Just when did H.H. get it? Do they know?"

Fidler looked at Andrew, for once waiting for him to answer. But Andrew's thoughts had been wandering and he started slightly, taking a moment to collect them. He had been thinking that for one thing Simon Kemp seemed to have a singular capacity for enjoying himself in what most people would have found trying circumstances and that perhaps he was the sort of person who ought to try to reach the North Pole on foot, or to climb some formidable mountain in mid-winter. Andrew himself had never felt the slightest inclination to undertake anything of the kind, but he could feel admiration for the people who were driven by some inner compulsion to do these unreasonable things.

"I don't think they can tell exactly when it happened," he said. "I had an appointment to meet Mr. Hewison in my cottage at five-thirty, but my train was very late and I didn't arrive till nearly an hour later. He was dying then—he died a few minutes after I found him—but he didn't manage to tell me who'd shot him, or when, so I don't know how long he'd been lying there. I presume he got into the cottage about the time we arranged, that's to say, about five-thirty."

"That's right," Fidler said. "It was just about five-thirty when I dropped him at your gate."

"It couldn't have been earlier?" There was a faint sound of anxiety in Kemp's voice.

"No, definitely not," Fidler said.

"Then Ruth's in the clear." Kemp stood up. "It was around

half past five when she came to see me and about six when
we set off for Croxley. And the people in the pub there can
say when we arrived and when she left. So that's all right.
Thanks for the coffee, Amabel. And let me know when you
want another bucketful of water."

"But good heavens, Simon, you don't mean to say you've
been suspecting Ruth!" Amabel exclaimed incredulously.
"D'you mean to say you've been thinking she might have
shot H.H. before she came to see you?"

He paused in the doorway. "No, of course not. Not exactly.
No, of course not. But I can't help wondering why she really
came. I don't understand it. Not that I've ever understood
her. Why did she marry me in the first place? I sometimes
ask myself that and I still don't know the answer. On the
rebound, was it, after that affair with Peter? Too late to
worry about it now, anyway. Be seeing you."

Soon after he had left, Andrew followed him out. He had
rung up the police station in Maddingleigh and made sure
that they had no objection to his reoccupying his home, and
so was able to return to Peter's cottage, carrying the few
belongings that he had brought with him the evening before. In the cottage he removed his shoes and began walking
about, as his habit was, in his socks, but the cold on his
unprotected feet made him look around hurriedly for his
slippers.

He found them in the living-room, under the coffee-table.
He also found a great deal of dust everywhere, which he
supposed was the result of a search for fingerprints, though
except for that the police had left the whole place pretty
tidy. He looked at the dust unhappily, thinking that in normal circumstances he would have been able to deal with it
fairly expeditiously with the vacuum cleaner. But that was as
useless to him now as the television, the electric fires and the
central heating.

The cottage felt far colder than the Fidlers'. No doubt that was because of all the coming and going that there had been in it the evening before, when doors had been left open and the little heat that might have been conserved in it had been wasted. Also the Fidlers had had a gas heater alight in their living-room, which had made it acceptably warm. Remembering the similar heater in Peter's garage, Andrew put on his shoes again and went out to the garage to bring the heater in.

It was on small wheels and was very heavy and there was not much hope of his being able to get it indoors unless he first cleared the path round the house of the snow that had fallen during the night. Taking a spade from the back of the garage where Peter stored his garden tools, Andrew went to work, digging a track clear of snow up to the front door. At least this was warming although after a little while his back began to ache, as it usually did these days if he stooped for more than a short time. It helped him if every few minutes he straightened up, massaged the base of his spine and took a few deep breaths. But at last the path was clear and he was able to wheel the heater into the house and along the passage to the living-room.

He did not know how the heater worked, but he found instructions under the lid at the top of it and turned the knob which they told him should set it alight. Nothing happened. He turned the knob again, tried turning every knob he could find, tried holding lighted matches to the burners, but still nothing happened. After about a quarter of an hour of futile effort, he gave it up. He knew what the trouble was. Peter had used up the gas in the cylinder inside the heater and then simply forgotten to have it replaced by a new one. Clearing the snow on the path had been a sheer waste of time. There was nothing for Andrew to do now but to wrap himself up well and endure the cold.

The incident made him think of Peter. Ought he not to

inform him of what had taken place in his home? On the whole he thought that he ought. That meant a telegram.

Going to the bureau, he found paper and a ball-point pen and composed one.

"Regret to inform you tragedy here last night Henry Hewison found shot in your living-room police in charge no clues yet as to murderer will remain here pending your instructions place bloody cold power cut no water best wishes New Year—Andrew."

He read this through carefully, then crossed out everything after the word "instructions" except his name and lifted the telephone.

It surprised him slightly that he heard the normal dialling tone. It was almost strange to find that one piece of apparatus in the cottage was functioning as it ought. After reading the message out to the operator, he replaced the telephone and began to think about lunch. Bread and cheese, he supposed, though it was a cheerless thought in this temperature. A hot meal would have been wonderful. But it would not help much to struggle against fate, and though he thought briefly of attempting a drive into Maddingleigh, where the evening before there had been no power cut, and seeing if he could get a good meal in a restaurant, he was nervous of taking the car out and down the steep drive to the main road and perhaps getting stuck in a drift somewhere. So bread and cheese it would have to be.

He went out to the kitchen and had just opened the refrigerator, which was merely a dark cavern, no colder than the rest of the house, when he heard the sound of a key being turned in the lock of the front door.

It was Mrs. Nesbit. She was dressed in the uniform of everyone he had seen during the last few days, an anorak with its hood up over her hair, trousers and boots. She was carrying a basket. Whatever it contained was wrapped in a towel. She brought it into the kitchen.

"Hallo, Mr. Basnett," she said. "How are you managing?"

"Not so badly so far," he answered. "I spent the night in the Fidlers' house, which is a good deal warmer than this. I only came back a short time ago. How are things with you?"

"Oh, we're fine," she said. "We've a good coal fire in the kitchen that heats the water, not that we dare draw off much from the tank so long as it's cut off at the main, but at least we can be sure it'll keep the pipes from freezing, and there's an oven over it where I've just cooked a chicken casserole. I brought some of it to you, as I knew you wouldn't have any way of cooking and you do want a nice hot meal on a day like this."

She put the basket down on the table, unwrapped the towel and revealed a casserole. Lifting it out of the basket, she went on, "Eat it while it's hot. I don't know if you care for chicken done like this with the potatoes and the vegetables and all mixed in, but it was the easiest way to do it in our oven."

"It sounds delicious," Andrew said. "How very kind of you."

"Well, we've got to help each other when things go wrong, haven't we?" she said. "You know, there's a Mrs. Greenaway living next door to us who's quite old, seventy at least, and of course she remembers the war and she said to me the freeze-up was bringing people together just like the air raids did in the war. From the way she said it, you'd almost think she'd enjoyed the air raids. Now do get on and eat this up before it gets cold."

"I can't thank you enough for this," Andrew said. "Altogether my neighbours have been very kind to me."

"It feels perishing in here," she said. "I'm sorry for you. Hasn't Mr. Dilly got a heater out in the garage?"

Andrew told her about the disaster with the heater. She nodded.

"That's what he's like. I always have to keep reminding

him of things. But he's nice to work for. I've been lucky with the people I work for. I get on with them all."

"I should think that's mostly because you're the sort of person you are," Andrew said. "You can take most of the credit."

"Oh, I don't know about that," she said, though she bridled and looked pleased. "Now do go on and eat. I'll pick up the casserole later today or perhaps tomorrow. I'll come in tomorrow, shall I? It isn't my day, but I must do something about all this terrible dust the police have left. D'you know, they came to see me this morning? It's terrible about poor Mr. Hewison, isn't it?"

Andrew sat down at the table and, since it seemed to be what she was anxious that he should do, began on the chicken.

"It is indeed," he said.

"I could start on the dust now, if you like," she said.

Andrew was not sure which she found the more terrible, the dust or the murder of Henry Hewison.

"I shouldn't bother about it till we've got the power back and you can use the vacuum cleaner," he said. "This chicken is excellent. What did the police want?"

She stood watching him eat. "Didn't Mr. Hewison speak about me just before he died?" she said.

"Yes, I told them that," Andrew answered. "But all I distinctly heard him say was your name."

"Well, that's what they came to see me about, about why he should have done that, and I think I know, as I told them, though I could be wrong. And now I can't help blaming myself for what happened, though I don't see how I was to know about it and I thought you wouldn't mind."

"I don't think I understand," Andrew said. "Why should you blame yourself for anything?"

"Well, it was me let him in, you see."

"Into the house?"

"That's right."

"How did that come about?"

She gave an uneasy sigh. Moving the towel which was still in the basket, she revealed that besides the casserole that it had contained, there was a thermos flask in it.

"I brought some coffee too," she said. "I'll have a cup myself, if you don't mind."

"Splendid," he said. "This is a positive feast. But about letting Mr. Hewison in . . . ?"

She brought two cups and saucers from the cupboard, filled one of the cups and, sitting down, nursing the cup in both hands, said, "I was sure you wouldn't mind, you see."

"I'm sure I shouldn't have," he said, "but what exactly did you do?"

"Well, I was on the bus coming back from Maddingleigh, where I'd been to see my sister," she said, "and I don't know if you've noticed it, but there's a bus-stop almost at your gate. The bus doesn't go down the lane to the village, it keeps straight on along the main road to Croxley, so the stop here's where I always get off. And I'd just got off when I saw Mr. Hewison get out of Mr. Fidler's car and go up the path to your door. And I knew you'd gone to London, so I thought perhaps you hadn't got home yet and he'd be standing there in the cold, waiting for you, not able to get in. There wasn't any light in your window, of course, but that didn't mean anything because all the lights around here had gone off already. Well, I waited a moment to see if you'd let him in, and I saw him ring the bell, but you didn't open the door, so I thought for sure you hadn't got home from London yet, and I thought the thing for me to do was to let him in, because of my having the key in my handbag, you see, and thinking it was what you'd want me to do. But if only I hadn't perhaps he wouldn't have been killed, I mean, because he'd simply have walked home again and the murderer wouldn't have found him, would he? So I can't help blaming myself."

"As you blamed yourself for his brother's murder," Andrew said. "You really mustn't do it." He was intent to reassure her, even though he could see that she felt some enjoyment at finding herself involved, if only on the fringe, in the drama of the murder. "But how were you able to see him ring my bell?"

"He shone his torch on it," she said.

"His torch?"

"That's right."

"You're sure of that? You're sure he had a torch?"

"Of course. I couldn't have seen what he did otherwise, could I?"

"No." It seemed to Andrew proof positive that Henry Hewison had had a torch when he arrived at the cottage, which meant, if the police had been unable to find it, that it might have been the torch which Pauline Hewison had been carrying when he had encountered her on the doorstep. And that would mean that she had been into the cottage before he found her and that only too probably it was she who had shot her brother-in-law.

"What time did this happen?" he asked.

"As near as I can say, a bit after half past five," Mrs. Nesbit answered. "The bus is supposed to stop here at five twenty-nine, but I know it was a little bit late yesterday because of the bad roads."

"D'you remember if Mr. Hewison used the torch as he came up the path, or only when he wanted to find the doorbell?"

She thought about it, then gave a slight shake of her head. "I couldn't say for certain. It was a very clear evening. I'd a torch of my own in my handbag, but I didn't bother to switch it on, I could see so well. So perhaps he didn't use it as he came up to the house. I didn't think about it."

Andrew reached for the thermos and poured out a cup of coffee for himself.

"But inside the house it was quite dark, was it?" he said.

"Oh yes."

"But Mr. Hewison didn't mind that?"

"No, he said he was sure the light would come on again any moment. He was wrong, of course, but that's how it usually is when we have a power cut. Sometimes it only lasts a few minutes, except if there's a strike or something like that. Why we have them at all I couldn't say, but this has always been a bad neighbourhood for it."

"Had you seen Mr. Hewison any time recently before yesterday?" Andrew asked.

"Well, not really," she said. "I mean, we just met in the village and had a chat. I've never known him well enough for more than that. I never worked for him or anything like that. But he was always ready to say good morning and ask how you were and that sort of thing."

"And you didn't see him and have one of those chats during the last day or two?" Andrew said.

"Yes, it happens I did. It was on Monday—no, that was Boxing Day, I didn't go out—it was Tuesday. We just met and wished each other a happy New Year."

"And chatted a bit?"

"That's right."

"Do you remember what you chatted about?"

She considered it again carefully. "In a way it's funny you should say that," she said, "because I talked, just like I did to you, about the chicken casserole I left in the oven for Mrs. Hewison the night her husband was killed. I didn't say much about it; I only said the snow had made me remember it and how I'd always wondered how she came to forget it. And he only said what you did, that she'd had other things on her mind."

"He wasn't much interested?"

"I can't say he was."

"Are you sure he wasn't?"

"I don't know just how I could say if I was *sure* or not. He didn't ask any special questions about it, if that's what you mean."

"I see."

Andrew did not see, but he thought it best to leave it at that. It did not sound as if the curious information that Henry Hewison had obtained, which he had wanted to discuss with Andrew, could have been connected with anything that Mrs. Nesbit had told him.

Yet her name had been the last word that the dying man had spoken.

When she had left, Andrew brooded for some time on her story of the casserole that had been left in the oven on the day of the first murder, to see if he could somehow connect the one with the other. But it seemed to him certain that Pauline Hewison, appalled and frightened at what had happened, had simply forgotten about the casserole and on becoming hungry later in the evening had not given it a thought, but had cooked herself some bacon and eggs.

There was a possibility, Andrew supposed, that Jack Fidler, taking Mrs. Nesbit's message on the telephone and promising to deliver it to Mrs. Hewison, had failed to do so. But why should he have done that? The Fidlers' telephone, Andrew had happened to notice, was in their living-room, where Fidler himself and Amabel and Pauline would have been playing their game of cutthroat, so he could hardly have forgotten the message between the time that he put the telephone down and the time that he rejoined the other two at the card-table. However, Andrew remembered, Pauline had been playing dummy at the time and just conceivably had been so engrossed in the game that when Fidler returned to it he had refrained from interrupting her until it was finished, and by then all memory of the message had disappeared from his mind.

Andrew knew that in similar circumstances he himself

could easily have forgotten what had been said to him only a
few minutes before, particularly if he had not really understood it in the first place. But Jack Fidler was a young man
with a brain not yet addled by old age, and who ought surely
to have been able to remember what Mrs. Nesbit had said to
him.

The warmth inside Andrew, generated by the meal that
he had eaten, did not last long. An intention that he had had
while he had been eating of doing some work that afternoon
did not survive the onset of acute cold that came soon afterwards. Going upstairs, he put on a heavy sweater under his
jacket, took a blanket downstairs with him, wrapped it
round his knees and settled down in a chair to read another
Agatha Christie novel that he had begun a day or two ago.
But he had no sooner begun on it than he recollected that
the daylight would not last much longer and that he had
done nothing yet about obtaining candles. He ought to
waste no more time now, sitting here, but should hurry
down to the village to buy some, or else go to one of his
neighbours to beg a few.

The trouble was, he felt so tired. He did not want to move.
All he really wanted to do at the moment was to have a little
sleep. He let his book sink onto his knees.

As he sat there, half-drowsing, words began to form at the
back of his mind.

> "There was a minnow went out for to winnow
> On Christmas Day, on Christmas Day,
> There was a minnow went out for to winnow
> On Christmas Day in the morning.
> There was a trout and he went out—"

But he put a stop to it there. He had never believed in the
authenticity of the trout. All the rest of the old Christmas
song related to farming activities, but the trout, he was sure,
had only been tagged on to the other verses at some later

date because of the convenience of the rhyme. Going back to the beginning of the song, he muttered softly:

"There was a pig went out to dig—"

Again he stopped abruptly. Nesbit. That had been the last word that Henry Hewison had spoken. But why should it be supposed to relate to Mrs. Nesbit. If there was a Mrs. Nesbit, there was a Mr. Nesbit too, wasn't there?

CHAPTER 6

That was Andrew's last conscious thought before he fell asleep. It was the ringing of the front doorbell that awakened him later. He was not sure that he had really heard a bell. It might have been something in a dream. There was twilight in the room. Wrapped in his blanket he felt fairly warm except for the cold on his face and he felt intensely reluctant to stir. But as he sat there, wondering if he really must, or if the sound of the bell had been imaginary, it rang again.

Disentangling himself from the blanket, he stood up. There was still light enough in the room for him to find his way to the door without difficulty, yet as he went a violent panic suddenly overcame him. He stood still and found that he was shivering, as much from fear as from the cold in the room. For had not Henry Hewison sat here in the darkness, waiting for Andrew's return, and on hearing the bell ring, as it had to be assumed he had, had gone to the door and allowed his murderer to enter? And suppose it was the murderer back again now, ringing the bell. Suppose he thought that Andrew had some information about the murder which made it important that he should be eliminated without delay. Suppose he was waiting out there on the doorstep with his gun in his hand.

But these thoughts went through Andrew's mind so

quickly that they hardly made him pause. As the fog of sleep receded, his panic faded. All the same, when he had gone down the passage to the front door and opened it, he was unreasonably relieved to see Godfrey Goodchild on the doorstep without any gun in his hand.

Though he was muffled up in a sheepskin jacket, his long, yellowish face looked pinched with the cold.

"I hope you don't mind—I mean, I hope I haven't interrupted you doing something important—but the fact is, Hannah and I have been worrying about you—knowing, I mean, that there's no way of heating this house till the electricity comes back on. We thought . . ." His extreme diffidence made him break off at that point, this thought of his and his wife's having apparently been too daring for him to express it. But after a brief hesitation he went on. "We thought you might care to come over to us. We thought you might—that's to say, if you aren't otherwise engaged—come over to supper with us. We've nothing much to offer you. Just some left-overs of our turkey. We always have a turkey at Christmas. Ridiculous, isn't it, as there are only the two of us, but we always do. And by the time we finish it we're so sick of it we can hardly bear the sight of it." He was talking faster and faster, as if, once he had got started, he did not know how to stop, a characteristic which Andrew had noticed before in very shy people. "Well, d'you feel like coming over? No need to, you know. If you'd sooner stay here on your own, just say so."

"I'd very much like to come over," Andrew said. "It's very kind of you to think of me. I don't seem able to stand the cold as well as I could when I was younger. Hypothermia, isn't that what it's called? The old suffer from it far worse than the young. And I've no way of cooking and actually I haven't even any candles. I meant to go into the village this afternoon to buy some, then I went to sleep instead."

"Good, good, then come along." Goodchild stamped his

feet on the hard-packed snow and shrugged his shoulders up to his ears. "Terrible about Hewison—terrible for you too, of course, having it happen here—but we won't talk about that now. I dare say you won't want to talk about it at all, but at least we can leave it till we get back to the fire."

Andrew changed out of his slippers into his shoes, put on his anorak and went with Goodchild down the path to the road. It was not quite dusk yet and even though Goodchild had brought no torch it was not too difficult for them to see their way. Goodchild led Andrew round the house to the back door, which opened as they approached it. Hannah had been watching for them. She was holding a candle, sheltering the flame of it with her hand from the draught from the door. There was a pleasant feeling of warmth in the big kitchen, for the old coal range had been lit. It made Andrew think of the kitchen of his childhood.

"Come in, come in," Hannah said. "I'm so glad you came. I told Godfrey, you must go and ask Professor Basnett to come over, because he must be freezing to death in that dreadful little house. We've always thought it dreadful, you know. It wasn't there when we came, or the Fidlers' either. There was just Simon's cottage, which is charming though it needs a lot done to it that he can't afford to do. Of course, he'd never have bought it if he hadn't got involved with that awful girl. A young man alone, like him, would be far better off in lodgings. Now come in to the fire."

She led the way to the sitting-room, where it was delightful to see a good fire burning in the grate. The room was lit by several candles and in their soft light had a look of shabby cosiness, far less dreary than in the bright sunshine in which Andrew had seen it last. Hannah was wearing the same dark blue dress that she had been wearing on that day and it struck Andrew that it was pleasant to see a woman in a skirt after the uniform of trousers and boots which all the others whom he had encountered recently had worn.

She stirred up the fire with the poker. "Come and sit down," she said, "and I think we'll have a drink. It's a little early for it perhaps, but in these conditions one loses one's sense of time. It doesn't seem to matter, does it? Godfrey, dear—sherry."

Andrew remembered with dismay the sherry that he had had on his last visit to the Goodchilds and there was no doubt about it, as he found when he sipped the drink that he was given, it came out of the same bottle. The peanuts too had been disinterred once more, but fortunately the cheesy things had been forgotten.

"Ah-h," he said, extending his feet to the blaze and hoping he sounded as if the sherry were as good as any he had ever tasted, "that makes one feel better. I wrapped myself up in a blanket and managed to have a nap this afternoon, but really the cold, going on and on like this, seems to get into the marrow of one's bones. But this will soon thaw me out."

"I don't like central heating," Hannah said. "I don't think it's healthy. I told Peter so when he was thinking of buying that house. 'You'll regret it,' I said, 'it makes the air too dry. You'll get bronchitis. There's nothing like a good open fire for health.' "

Andrew had never heard that bronchitis was a probable result of central heating and having lived with it himself for many years would not have returned for anything to the tyranny of keeping one of those good open fires going. The last twenty-four hours was the first time in his experience when he had suffered for the lack of one, and with luck, he thought, he might reach the fires of the crematorium before it happened again.

But he recognized the tone of confirmed prejudice when he heard it. The most unfruitful thing possible would be to enter into an argument with Hannah Goodchild on the matter, or perhaps on any matter whatever.

"Now tell us everything about this dreadful thing that

happened last night," she said. "The police have been to see us, of course, because of our coming over to your house, but on the whole they were very uncommunicative. They asked us a lot of questions but they didn't tell us anything, so Godfrey and I don't really know much about what happened, except that you found Mr. Hewison lying there, dying."

"Dear," her husband said, "we don't know that Professor Basnett wants to talk about it. He's probably had to do more than enough of that already. I'm sure we can find something else to talk about."

"What, for instance?" she asked.

That seemed to defeat him. He had sat down in a chair, leaning back so that he was lying almost flat in it, with his long legs stretched out before him. Nursing his sherry glass on his chest, he shook his head slightly as if he had lost this argument before and had given in.

"It was strange," Andrew said. "He said something just before he died."

"He spoke—he actually spoke?" Hannah said with sudden eagerness.

"Yes, he said just one word," Andrew answered. " 'Nesbit.' "

" 'Nesbit'?" she said. "That *is* strange."

"Do you know the Nesbits?" Andrew asked.

"Oh yes, I meet Mrs. Nesbit quite often at the Women's Institute. A very nice woman."

"And Mr. Nesbit?"

"Oh, he's very nice too. He's a joiner and a very clever one and doesn't charge exorbitantly if you pay him in cash. He's done a few jobs for us, put up some shelves and things like that."

"Do you think there's any chance he had a grudge of some sort against Mr. Hewison?"

The Goodchilds exchanged puzzled looks.

"I can't imagine why he should have," Hannah said.

"Have you any evidence he had?" Goodchild asked.

"None at all," Andrew said. "It's just this strange thing about the last word that Hewison spoke having been 'Nesbit.' I took for granted at first it meant Mrs. Nesbit. She told me this morning it was she who let Hewison into the house, so I thought that might be why she was on his mind. Then it occurred to me later that there's a Mr. Nesbit and that he'd been doing a job of work up at the school, putting up some bookshelves. So I wondered what kind of man he was. Cantankerous, unstable, liable to bear a grudge?"

"Anything but, I should say," Goodchild said. "Don't you agree, Hannah?"

"Oh yes, indeed," she said. "Just a very steady, conscientious craftsman. I'm sure he's a very good husband. You can tell from the way Mrs. Nesbit speaks of him. So he was doing some work for Mr. Hewison, was he? I believe he did some for the other Mr. Hewison too, putting up shelves or something, just before he was killed. That's how the Nesbits met one another. Mrs. Nesbit was housekeeper at Godlingham House at the time and he had to go up there day after day for a bit and it didn't take them long to decide they wanted to get married."

"I wonder . . ." Goodchild said.

"Yes?" Andrew said after a moment's silence in which it seemed that Goodchild did not mean to expound his thoughts any further.

"Nothing," he said. "Just an idea. I thought for a moment . . . no, it's nothing."

"Godfrey often has ideas," Hannah said with the tenderness she might have used if she had been speaking of a child. "Very good ideas some of them are too, but it's no use trying to hurry him. He'll tell you about it when he's ready."

"It's just that I wondered if Nesbit's been seeing Hewison recently," Goodchild said, "if he might have told him something he'd noticed at Godlingham House when he was working there that Hewison somehow connected with his brother's murder. And if he'd talked indiscreetly about it, well, it might explain . . ." He left the sentence unfinished.

"Something Nesbit's kept to himself for six years?" Hannah said. "Is that likely? Some more sherry, Professor?"

Little as Andrew had enjoyed it, it was at least helping the fire to drive the chill out of his blood and he thanked her and held out his glass. Goodchild pulled himself up from his reclining position onto his feet to refill it.

"Of course I told the police about seeing that woman go up the path to your house," Hannah said when her glass had been refilled too.

"That woman? Mrs. Nesbit?" Andrew asked.

"No, no, no, the Hewison woman."

"Hannah," her husband said quickly, "I told you you shouldn't say that. You shouldn't have told the police. You couldn't possibly be sure."

"But I *was* sure," she said. "I saw her. I saw her as clear as day."

"When was this?" Andrew asked.

"Yesterday evening," she said. "About a quarter to six, perhaps."

"It wasn't later than that?"

"I don't think so. I know I'd absent-mindedly tried to switch on the five-forty news, forgetting the television wouldn't work any more than the lights would, and when nothing happened I realized how stupid I'd been and switched it off again and went to the window to draw the curtains. And because the stars were so bright and because we'd no light in this room I could see outside quite clearly and I saw Mrs. Hewison walk up the path to your door. Yes, it would have been about a quarter to six."

"Was she carrying a torch?"

"No, you could see so well you really didn't need one."

"And did you see me drive up a minute or two later?"

"No. Did you get in about then?"

"I think it was rather later," Andrew said. "My train was three quarters of an hour late and didn't get into Maddingleigh till about half past five and I'm sure it took me more than a quarter of an hour to get home."

"Well, that explains why I didn't see you," she said. "I didn't stay at the window long, two or three minutes, perhaps, because the snow was so beautiful in the starlight. Then I just drew the curtains and went out to the kitchen to see what I could do about supper. And that reminds me, we're only going to give you turkey sandwiches and open a tin of prunes. I do hope Godfrey explained to you I'm not doing any more cooking than I can help. We've got the stove lit in the kitchen for the sake of the warmth, but I don't really know how to cook on it."

"That'll be fine," Andrew said. "Your fire alone is a treat. But going back to Mrs. Hewison, you're sure you saw her go up the path to my door some time before I arrived?"

"She can't be sure," Goodchild interposed with the same anxious haste as before. "She saw someone go up the path, but however bright it was outside, she couldn't have told from this distance who it was. For instance, it could have been Ruth. She and her mother are very alike. When you see them together Ruth's a little the taller, but they're very similar in build."

"I believe that at the time we're talking about Ruth was in Croxley, or on the way there," Andrew said. "She and Kemp went to the pub there and had a quarrel and she walked out on him and drove home, leaving him to walk back. There'll be witnesses in the pub to say what time they arrived and when she left, and I don't think it's likely she was here at a quarter to six. What I'm interested in is whether Mrs. Hewison went up to the cottage more than a minute or two before I got there."

"Well, I saw her quite clearly go up to it at about a quarter to six and I didn't see you arrive at all," Hannah said, "so she was there well ahead of you, if that's what's on your mind. Oh, it's so obvious what happened, isn't it? She saw Mrs. Nesbit let Mr. Hewison into the house and she knew you hadn't got home and he let her in and she shot him and when you saw her she'd just come out; she wasn't trying to get in. I don't think there's any doubt of it."

"But why should she shoot him?" Andrew asked.

"Because he'd found out something about the murder of her husband, of course."

"And told her he had?"

"He must have, mustn't he, or she wouldn't have known she needed to silence him?"

"I do wish you'd be quiet, Hannah," her husband said fretfully. "This is all pure speculation. You can't really be sure it was Mrs. Hewison you saw. You can't be sure what the exact time was. You can't be sure how long you were at the window and you can't be sure Professor Basnett didn't drive up the moment you drew the curtains. You're only making trouble, saying these things, for us probably as well as for Pauline Hewison."

"Well, I'll tell you one thing I'm absolutely sure of," she said, "and you'll never argue me out of it. That woman's wicked. People like her don't change. They're born wicked and they stay wicked to the end. Don't tell me anything about deprived childhoods and so on, it's something that's in them from the beginning and there's no curing it. It's a thing I've always felt when I've had to meet her. Not that I didn't avoid her almost from the time they first arrived here, as you know, but sometimes in the old days, when she used to go about more, I couldn't help meeting her at the Women's Institute or in other people's houses, and then I believe I was always courteous. But I could always feel her wickedness in my bones. You'll never get me to change my mind about her."

The passion with which she spoke seemed to embarrass Goodchild, for he coughed uneasily and said, "Yes, well . . . I don't like to condemn anybody . . . People do change, whatever you say. About those sandwiches now . . ."

She stood up and reached for a candle, preparing to go out to the kitchen.

But before she went, there was one question that Andrew wanted to ask and to which he thought he was more likely to obtain an answer from her than from her husband.

"She must have been very young when Ruth was born," he said. "She told me herself Ruth is illegitimate, but surely it must have happened when Mrs. Hewison was a mere child."

Hannah laughed harshly. "Below the age of consent, you mean. You can be quite sure she was. Fourteen or fifteen at the most. You can tell that just by looking at the two of them. It's what I was telling you, the woman was corrupt from the start. Now I'll make those sandwiches. And give Professor Basnett some more sherry, Godfrey."

This time Andrew declined the sherry and when Hannah had gone out to the kitchen he and Goodchild had a peaceful chat about matters unconnected with murder. The subject of archaeology was introduced by Goodchild and in talking about it he became quite animated. It appeared that there was an archaeological society in the village, of which he was chairman, and that there were various tombs, stone circles and even the remains of a Roman villa not far away, which were generally considered noteworthy. He offered to take Andrew on a tour of inspection of some of them when the weather should have improved. But apart from this he dropped no clues as to what his profession, if any, had been when he was younger, or where he and Hannah had lived before coming to Godlingham, more than twenty years ago.

It was almost as if he and his wife had only come into existence at that time, suddenly ejected into their present way of life from outer space. It was difficult to think of him as ever having been anything but elderly, except that now and then, when he smiled or when he was describing with enthusiasm some tumulus or other relic, Andrew caught a glimpse of the handsome man that he must have been once before bitter experience, or possibly illness, had ravaged his face.

It was perhaps not tactful of Andrew, but later in the evening, when the sandwiches and the tinned prunes had been eaten and some very watery coffee had been drunk and he was in the kitchen, with the back door standing open and Goodchild holding a candle up so that Andrew could see his way out, he could not resist saying, "Tell me, Mr. Goodchild, if it isn't impertinent of me to ask, but aren't you a doctor?"

The candle wobbled and the shadows it cast leapt wildly about the room.

In an unusually strident voice Goodchild answered, "No, I am not a doctor. No, certainly not!"

"I only asked because of the way you lifted Hewison's eyelid and shone your torch in his eye," Andrew said. "A layman like me would never have thought of doing that."

"I am not a doctor," Goodchild repeated with his voice even louder. "I am nothing. I am nobody. If ever I was anybody once, I prefer not to remember it. It's all over long ago."

Slamming the candle down on the table, he turned and stalked out of the kitchen, leaving Andrew alone in it.

He was not sure what he was expected to do, but after a moment, as there was no sound of returning footsteps, he left the candle alight where it was, stepped through the door, closed it behind him and set off cautiously in the darkness towards the gate. It was not as difficult as he had thought it would be. It was another very clear night with stars in their cold, brilliant remoteness shining brightly in the black vault of the sky and with some of their light reflected by the snow, so that the pathway to the gate was clearly visible.

Half-way down the path he paused and looked at Peter's cottage.

Yes, he thought as he stood there, it was just possible that if Hannah Goodchild had been looking out of her window when Pauline Hewison had been walking up to the cottage, Hannah might have recognized her. He did not feel sure about it, but he thought that she just might have been able to do so. It could not be ruled out. Then he thought of the passion of hatred there had been in her voice when she had accused Pauline of wickedness. Walking on again, he found himself caught once more in the spell woven by the witches in Macbeth and shuddered slightly. Positively, he thought his own thumbs were pricking a little. At all events, he had never felt before as he did just then that there was wickedness in the atmosphere. But from whence did it come? Who was it that was affecting his thumbs in that unpleasant fashion?

Reaching the gate, he opened it, stepped out into the road, slipped on an icy patch and fell down.

He did not hurt himself. He felt a jarring of his spine and a bruise on his knee, but neither was serious and he was able to pick himself up and continue along the road to his gate. He walked almost in the ditch, where the snow had not been flattened by the small amount of traffic that had passed along the road that day and had not been frozen hard. He was about to turn in at his gate when a thought came to him suddenly, made him pause for a moment, then continue along the road to the Fidlers' gate. He walked up the path to their door and rang the bell.

Amabel opened the door.

"Oh, I'm so glad you've come," she said, warmly welcoming him in, then hurriedly closing the door behind him to keep out the cold. "Jack went round to you earlier this evening to see how you were managing, but he said there wasn't any answer. We've been a little worried about you. You've been all right, have you?"

"Perfectly all right," Andrew answered. "I've been having supper with the Goodchilds. Everyone here is looking after me so well, I feel immensely grateful. I came round partly because I wondered if you could spare me a candle. I ought to have thought of it sooner and gone to the village to buy some, but I went to sleep instead. Then there's something else I wanted to ask you, just something I'm curious about."

"We've plenty of candles," Amabel said. "But come in and get warm. We've had our radiator going all day and we're terrified the gas will give out at any moment, but it's been all right so far and we're fairly comfortable. If it does give out Jack will take the cylinder into Maddingleigh to change it tomorrow. What about yours? I remember Peter had one. Is it functioning all right?"

"I'm afraid it isn't functioning at all," Andrew said. "Either I don't understand it, or the gas has run out and I'm afraid I don't know what I ought to do about it. I'm not accustomed to these things."

"You just get the cylinder exchanged." Amabel led the way into the sitting-room. "Jack will see to it for you when he takes ours in. Jack, Professor Basnett's gas has run out and I was just saying you'll take his cylinder into Maddingleigh tomorrow to get him a fresh one."

Fidler got to his feet from a chair close to the radiator.

"Of course—if the power still hasn't come on again. I've been phoning the electricity people and giving them hell, but you'd think they weren't even interested."

"I suppose so many people have been ringing up and giving them hell," Andrew said, "that they've developed a certain immunity to it. I was just telling your wife, I came over to see if you'd a candle you could spare and also to ask you something about which I'm a little puzzled."

"Sit down then and have a drink," Fidler said. "I think I heard you tell Amabel you'd been having supper with the Goodchilds. In that case you could probably stand a strong whisky."

Andrew admitted that he could. As he sat down near to the radiator Fidler went to the sideboard and made drinks for the three of them. The room was lit by an old oil-lamp, which looked as if it had spent a long time unused in a cupboard, yet which shed a brighter light than the candles on which the Goodchilds were relying.

"Isn't it strange how adaptable human beings are," Andrew said as he accepted a glass of whisky and soda from Fidler. "A week or two of this and we'd be taking it for granted and forgetting that we'd ever lived differently. I almost feel it would give me a shock if the lights suddenly came on."

"All the same, it's a scandal," Fidler proclaimed in his resonant voice. "Here we are only forty minutes by train from London and having to live as if we were in the Arctic. What is it you wanted to ask us about?"

"I'm afraid it's sheer inquisitiveness on my part," Andrew said, "but an odd thing happened when I was at the Goodchilds and I wondered if you could explain it to me. Am I right, do you know, that Goodchild's a doctor?"

Fidler gave an abrupt laugh. "Yes, he is."

"Then why is he so sensitive about having it known? I asked him if he was and it seemed to give the deepest offence."

"Oh, it would, it would," Fidler said. "But what gave you the idea that he might be one?"

Andrew told him and Amabel how he had seen Goodchild ascertain that Henry Hewison was dead by lifting his eyelid and shining a torch into his eye.

Fidler nodded. "More or less the way we stumbled on it ourselves," he said. "Amabel had a fall in the garden and thought she'd broken her wrist and Godfrey was in his garden and heard her yell and came round to see what had happened. And the way he handled her wrist and said it wasn't broken but only sprained was so professional, we were sure he must have had at least some medical training."

"And he has?"

"Oh yes. More than that. As a matter of fact—"

"Jack!" Amabel said in a warning tone, as if she did not want him to say any more.

He laughed again. "Why shouldn't I tell the story? Professor Basnett isn't likely to go gossiping about it around the village. We only found out about it ourselves because after that affair with Amabel's wrist we were curious about it and looked into it. The fact is, Godfrey was struck off the medical register for grossly unprofessional conduct. It's difficult to imagine, isn't it, dried-up old character that he is? But that's the truth."

"You're implying it was sexual misconduct," Andrew said.

"Oh, of course. He got a girl of fifteen pregnant when she was a patient of his. It was more or less rape, I gathered. But that isn't the whole story—"

"Jack!" Amabel interrupted again. "Please!"

Fidler gave a kind of giggle. Nothing would stop him now. Andrew wondered how many drinks he had had before his arrival.

"I don't know if you can guess the rest of the story," Fidler said. "Who was the girl? Well, you know her. Her name was Pauline Hockley. And to begin with she refused to name Godfrey as the father, it was her mother who brought the case, and after a bit Pauline gave in and admitted it. It ruined Godfrey's career, of course, and he's never done anything else since. He's just a wreck of a man. I suppose he and Hannah had a little money and they came to live here after the thing happened, and he'll deny it to your face that he was ever a doctor. But I've seen the records and I know."

"So he's Ruth's father, is he?" Andrew said. "Mrs. Hewison told me it was a man in the Army."

"And that may be the truth."

"You think she accused him falsely?"

"I'm inclined to think she did, though I've no proof of it."

"But why should she do that?"

"Pressure from her mother, perhaps. She was just a child. Or some idea that Godfrey would look after her when she'd been deserted by the child's real father. Of course he didn't."

"Professor Basnett, please!" Amabel insisted on being heard. "This is three quarters guesswork. It's true Godfrey was a doctor and was struck off the register and that it was because he was supposed to have got a patient of his pregnant and the girl was Pauline, but that's absolutely all we know. And I wish Jack hadn't told you that much. If you hadn't asked that question straight out about whether or not Godfrey was a doctor we'd never have said a thing about it. You sort of took us by surprise. But I know we can rely on you not to tell the story to anyone else."

Andrew felt oddly reluctant to give her this reassurance. The story might be one, he thought, which sooner or later would have to be told to the police. He did not see why it should be, except that everything to do with Pauline Hewison had in his mind a flavour of ambiguity. But he wanted to reserve his option to tell it if it should become desirable.

"I understand now why Mrs. Goodchild has such a hatred of Mrs. Hewison," he said. "It rather puzzled me before. How was it they came to meet here? Was it just by chance?"

Fidler nodded. "Sheer bloody misfortune. The Good-childs had been living here for years before Charles Hewison bought Godlingham House. In a small island like this it's the kind of thing that happens much more often than people realize. Think how often you meet people you know in the middle of London by accident. The Hewisons came here, of course, to be near H.H., and I don't believe Godfrey even recognized Pauline at first, though I think she knew him immediately. There's a much bigger change between a child of fifteen and a woman of thirty-five than between a man of forty or thereabouts and one of sixty. I remember he told me soon after the Hewisons came here how nice they were and how pleasant it was going to be having people like them at Godlingham House. But one of the first times I ever met Pauline she had a ferocious row with her husband in front of a number of people, telling him that nothing would make her stay in Godlingham, and though she didn't explain it at the time, she was so hysterical that I've come to believe it was because she couldn't bear settling down to live just across the road from someone she'd wronged so frightfully."

"Or who had wronged her," Amabel said. "You really don't know the truth about that."

"How did the Goodchilds find out who she was?" Andrew asked.

"I've an idea it was through Ruth," Fidler answered. "She's got a way of telling people her name's Hockley, al-most boasting about the fact that she's illegitimate, and if she did that to the Goodchilds of course they'd have remem-bered the name and once they started thinking about it they may have recognized Pauline."

"Do you know that Mrs. Goodchild claims to have seen Mrs. Hewison go up to my door at least some minutes before I arrived?" Andrew said. "And that she didn't have a torch. If Mrs. Goodchild has told that to the police, Mrs. Hewison is going to be in an unfortunate position."

The Fidlers looked at one another and an expression of shock appeared on both their faces.

"But that's impossible!" Amabel exclaimed. "How could Hannah see her in the dark?"

"Particularly if Pauline hadn't got a torch," her husband said.

"Nevertheless, Mrs. Goodchild insists she could see her quite plainly in the starlight," Andrew said.

"Then she's trying to frame her!" Fidler cried. He sprang to his feet, went to the sideboard and poured out another whisky for himself. "Amabel's right, it wouldn't be possible."

"I'm not sure I agree with you," Andrew said. "When I was walking back from their house I took a look towards my cottage and I thought she just might have been able to see someone walk up the path."

"Someone, perhaps, but not recognize who it was!" Fidler was almost shouting. "It's a frame-up, revenge, because of how they hate her. We've got to stop it. We've got to do something about it."

"But what?" Andrew asked.

Fidler returned to his chair and sat down, scowling. "Find out who it really was," he said.

"Isn't that a matter for the police?"

"Of course, of course. But if the Goodchilds are going to tell them something like that she's hardly got a chance, has she?"

"You're quite sure it couldn't have been her they saw?"

"Yes, I'm sure. Listen." Fidler gulped some of his whisky, then leant forward, sawing the air with one finger, as if he were delivering a lecture to a disorderly class. "For Pauline Hewison to have killed H.H. she'd have had to have a motive, wouldn't she? And what motive could she have had? That he'd found out something that involved her in her husband's murder? That was what H.H. was always trying to find. But I can tell you—yes, *I*—" He thumped himself on the chest. "I can tell you she was here with us when he was killed. Other people may not believe us, but *we* know she was! Amabel and I know she was here and is absolutely innocent. We know for certain she'd no reason to kill H.H. and if the Goodchilds say so, they're lying."

His voice had risen again, so that he was shouting into Andrew's face as if he were sitting in the back row of a large class-room. After it, Amabel's voice sounded soothingly gentle.

"Professor Basnett, I want to ask you something which I think may make you very angry," she said.

He blinked a little, trying to recover from the effects of Jack Fidler's roaring.

"I'm sure you won't," he said. "What is it?"

"It's something I've really no right to ask," she said, "but I can't help wondering, what kind of relationship is there between you and Peter?"

It did not make Andrew angry, it only bewildered him. He looked at her in astonishment. He was unable to guess what could possibly have made her ask the question. He found her looking steadily at him from under her level brows and it occurred to him that, quiet as she was, there was far more strength in her than in her blustering husband. Indeed, it might be her strength that kept her as quiet as she was. She might be so sure of herself that she felt no need to compete with his noisy self-assertion.

"A very good relationship," he said. "We're the best of friends."

"And he's nothing to gain by your death?"

He began to understand her drift now and he felt the first dull heat of anger inside him, but he was determined not to let it show. He sounded almost indifferent as he answered, "In my will I've left everything I possess to him. But that isn't a great deal. My university pension will stop at my death and so will my old-age pension, and all I have besides those are some modest investments and the flat I own. And that wouldn't mean a great deal to Peter. Since his success with his science fiction, he's a great deal richer than I am."

"Are you sure of that?" she asked.

"Yes, of course I'm sure," he said, though with a sudden sinking of the heart he realized that the only evidence of it that he had was what Peter himself had told him.

"There, I knew I'd make you angry," she said sadly, "though I'll be the first to admit I'm talking nonsense. All the same, I do think perhaps I ought to tell you what's on my mind, just so that you can tell me what nonsense it is. And if the police raise the matter, we'll know what to say about it." She had planted her elbows on her knees and was holding her face between her hands with her eyes still steadily on Andrew. "You see, H.H. was killed in the dark, wasn't he? So isn't it possible he was killed by mistake? Just think what happened. He was in there in the house, waiting for you, and I imagine he was in your sitting-room, and then someone— his murderer—came to the door. Perhaps whoever it was rang the bell. If that happened, I imagine H.H. would have got up and gone to answer it, but if he'd done that wouldn't one of two things have happened? Either he'd have opened the door and the murderer would have shot him on the spot, in which case he'd have collapsed on the floor by the front door, or else, not suspecting trouble of any kind because it was someone he knew, he'd have let him in and led him along to the sitting-room, in which case his murderer might not have shot him till he got to the doorway, where the police told Jack he was found, but all the same he'd almost certainly have been shot in the back before he turned round. But we understand he was facing his murderer when he was shot, that the bullet hit him in the chest, just missing his heart, which is why he didn't die instantly. So we can be sure neither of those things happened."

"Well?" Andrew said.

"Well, mightn't it all have happened quite differently?" she said, her tone apologetic, as if it distressed her to offend him. "Imagine H.H. sitting there in the dark, then hearing a key turn in the lock of the front door. He'd have got up, wouldn't he, and gone to the door of the sitting-room to see who it was? And he and his murderer might then have met in the doorway. Then the shot might have been fired at this tall figure standing there in the pitch-darkness before the murderer had time to realize who it was. I'm supposing, you see, that he thought it was you, because apart from Mrs. Nesbit, the only person I can think of who has a key to that cottage is Peter, and he's the only person who belongs hereabouts who could conceivably have a reason to kill you."

Andrew said nothing. In spite of the fact that the room was reasonably warm and that the Fidlers' whisky had driven out the chill with which he had arrived, he felt as if he had begun to shiver, although when he looked at the hand that was holding his glass it was quite steady. At last he stood up.

"I think I'd better go home," he said.

"There, I knew I'd make you angry," Amabel said. "But why don't you just tell us it's nonsense and sit down and have another drink?"

"It's nonsense," he said.

"Then have another drink."

"No, thank you. I'll say good night and thank you for your hospitality. And if the police ask you any questions, just tell them what you've said to me. It'll be a good thing to have the matter out in the open and get it cleared up. I've no doubt at all that Peter will be able to prove he was in Paris at the relevant time."

Without waiting to be shown out, Andrew made for the Fidlers' door.

He was half-way home before he realized that he and they

had forgotten about the candle that they had promised him, so he would have to go to bed in the dark.

It was not as difficult as he had anticipated. He knew his way about the cottage fairly well by now and was able to collect some blankets from the spare bedroom and heap them on his bed, undress and then crawl into it and hope that his own body warmth would soon make the cold sheets feel less inhospitable. He felt a craving for a hot bath, but this now seemed to him a luxury which possibly he might never enjoy again. Never, that was to say, unless he packed up tomorrow and went back to London. The thought of this began to attract him more and more. Even the presence of decorators in his flat began to seem a small discomfort compared with what he was enduring here. They would at least depart in the evenings and he would then be able to sit alone in his cosily heated flat, have one hot bath after another if he chose, cook himself steaks and chops or whatever took his fancy without having to depend on the generosity of his neighbours and revel in sybaritic peace. How wonderful it sounded.

But would the police let him go? Would they not, probably with the utmost politeness, request that he should remain in Godlingham, at least until after the inquest? And being a good citizen, would he not do as they asked without any argument?

Some time while he was turning these matters over in his mind, he fell asleep.

Perhaps reluctant to emerge from the bed, which had eventually grown warm, he woke a little later than usual the next morning. There was already daylight in the room and he was able to see by his watch that it was a quarter to eight. But as he lay there, nerving himself to get up, he realized that it was not the daylight that had wakened him. It had been the sound of someone moving about downstairs.

Getting quickly out of bed, fumbling his way into his

dressing-gown, he dashed out of his room to the top of the stairs.

"Who's there?" he shouted.

"It's all right," the voice of Peter Dilly answered, "it's only me."

CHAPTER 7

Andrew went back into his bedroom, put socks on his feet and went downstairs. He found Peter fiddling ineffectively with the gas heater.

"I'm sorry about this," Peter said, "I haven't had to use it since I bought it six years ago. I suppose the gas has gradually leaked away. I'll take the cylinder into Maddingleigh and get a new one."

"The Fidlers said they'd do that for me," Andrew said. "How did you get here?"

"Taxi from Heathrow," Peter answered.

"That must have cost you quite a bit."

"Yes, well, if I'd taken the bus to Reading and then a train to Maddingleigh and then a taxi from the station to God-lingham, it would have cost almost as much and taken twice the time. I came on the early plane. I thought I ought to do that as soon as I got your telegram." Peter abandoned the gas heater and, straightening up, thrust back his tumbled hair from his forehead. "You know, when I persuaded you to come down here I thought I could guarantee you peace and comfort. I'm afraid you haven't had much of either. I'm very sorry about it. What can we do about breakfast? We can't boil a kettle, can we?"

Andrew had bought some cans of beer earlier in the week

and suggested that they should open a couple and eat some bread and marmalade.

"After all, Mr. Pickwick used to drink beer for breakfast," he said. "He also ate roast beef and I'm sorry I can't offer you that, but it's only habit that makes us think we have to have tea or coffee. I've been thinking a lot about habit during the last day or two and how one allows it to dominate one's existence as one gets old. It makes one take so much for granted which we did without even as recently as my own childhood, though I suppose that sounds a very long time ago to you. Peter, what sort of people are the Fidlers?"

Peter looked puzzled. "They're all right. Why?"

"You're on good terms with them?"

"I should say so, yes. Jack's a bit of a bore, but Amabel's quite good value once you get to know her. Have they got across you somehow?"

"They've been extremely good to me. But yesterday evening Amabel came up with a rather good theory to prove it was probably you who murdered Hewison in mistake for me. Oddly enough, I thought she was serious and I started wondering how good friends you were with them. I suppose you can prove you were in Paris yesterday evening."

Peter's smile lit up his normally rather blank face. "What do you think yourself?"

"You don't have to ask me that, you know that. But could you prove where you were to the police, for instance?"

"Well, I think I can. I was alone, but I had dinner in a café where I think I'll be remembered because of my atrocious French. If the people there didn't notice me, I can't swear to it that anyone else did."

"It's a pity they don't bother to stamp your passport any more as you come in and out of the country," Andrew said. "If they did that you'd have an unassailable alibi. Now let's have breakfast, such as it is, then we can consider what to do about the gas for that heater. I've a feeling that the moment you buy a new cylinder the power will come on again."

"How long has it been off?" Peter asked.

"Since some time on Thursday afternoon. I don't know just when. I was in London when it happened."

Andrew went out to the kitchen, ate his usual small ration of cheese, then opened two cans of beer and emptied them into glasses, put bread, butter and marmalade on a tray and carried it into the sitting-room. Peter had kept on his overcoat and was sitting with it huddled around him in one of the chairs. A beam of sunlight, coming in at the big window, lit up the dust that had been spilled over everything by the police.

Drinking some beer, Peter said, "Well, tell me all about it."

Andrew did so, beginning with Henry Hewison's telephone call to him to ask if he could come to the cottage to discuss some curious information he had obtained with someone who would be dispassionate, and ending, after talking about Pauline Hewison, her daughter, Simon Kemp, the Goodchilds and, finally, the Fidlers, with a repetition of Amabel Fidler's attempt to cast doubts on Peter's innocence.

"And that brings me back to what I asked you a little while ago," Andrew said. "What kind of people are the Fidlers?"

"You mean what they've got against me, seeing they seem so keen to drag me into the thing," Peter said. "I've never known they had anything against me. I think it must be that they're truly anxious to protect Pauline, if things are looking black for her."

"No, that isn't exactly what I meant," Andrew said. "I was thinking about their story about Godfrey Goodchild."

"Is it true, d'you mean?"

"No, I'm sure it's true. Fidler was very positive about it. I don't think he'd have risked telling me anything like that unless he could back it up with evidence. But what kind of man is it who would go to all the trouble of digging up the dirt in an old story like that? A very old story, if Pauline Hewison was only fifteen at the time. It must have been quite difficult to get the facts. Yet when he became suspicious that Goodchild was a doctor because of the way he handled Amabel's wrist when she thought she'd broken it, Fidler didn't simply leave it at that, as most of us would have done, but investigated the whole thing and then told me, a relative stranger, all about it. I felt at the time there was something queer about his doing that, and the more I think about it, the odder it seems."

"You were pretty curious about it yourself, weren't you, when you began to suspect Godfrey was a doctor and was keeping very quiet about it?" Peter said.

"Yes, I was curious," Andrew admitted. "But I'd never have taken the matter any further. I'd never have gone hunting through old records to try to get something on the man. And I can't help feeling that that's what Fidler must have been doing—trying to get something on Goodchild which he could somehow use against him."

Peter spread some marmalade on a piece of bread and butter. The bread had become more than a little stale since Andrew bought it.

"I'd say Jack told you about Godfrey and his murky past to show you that Hannah had a motive for trying to frame Pauline. And perhaps the way Jack hunted up that old case originally had something to do with protecting her from some threat from the Goodchilds, though I can't see just how that could have worked."

"Do you believe in Goodchild's murky past?" Andrew said.

"I assume there was a case against him if he was struck off the medical register as a result of it," Peter said. "But whether or not he was guilty is another matter."

"If he wasn't, then Mrs. Hewison lied about it."

"Perhaps she did. I find that easier to believe than that a man like Godfrey raped, or at least seduced, a child. But I've told you, I've always felt there was something strange about Pauline."

"But why are the Fidlers so determined to protect her? They seem to be hardly friends. On her side, I'd say, there's active dislike."

"Perhaps they let her know they knew her history and perhaps she couldn't bear that."

"In that case, why has she stayed on here all these years? You'd think the mere presence of the Goodchilds would have made her move away when her husband died, and if the Fidlers knew the story too and that upset her, it would be another reason for moving."

"I know. It's always puzzled me why she stayed."

"Fidler dropped a hint that Hewison had some hold on her," Andrew said, "something to do with being able to prove she killed her husband, and that now he was dead perhaps she'd go. He also had an idea that with her brother-in-law out of the way and someone else in charge of the school, she might be persuaded to put some money into it and save it. Hewison himself told me he was going to have to close it for lack of funds. D'you think there's anything in that?"

Peter looked dubious. "I don't think it sounds particularly likely. She's never taken any interest in the school."

"What's so special about the place?" Andrew asked. "Is it really worth saving?"

"It was special to H.H. simply because it was his," Peter answered. "Apart from that, I don't think education would suffer a deadly blow if it folded."

Andrew gave a sudden grin. "H.H. was the model for your Camellords, wasn't he? I recognized him as soon as I saw him."

"Actually, no," Peter said. "They were based a good deal

more on his brother Charles. H.H. was really a rather gentle
old thing, quite modest, with nice vague ideas about how he
was going to produce a superbly educated aristocracy of the
kind required in the present technological age. But I think
most of the ideas he ever had were his brother's. He was a
truly arrogant, domineering man who looked even more
like a camel than H.H. But he hadn't the humanity in him to
be able to handle children himself, so all he did was preach
to his brother and make him do what he wanted."

"You're making him sound the sort of man whom a wife
might want to murder."

"Yes, he was that."

"Which brings us back to the Fidlers and the alibi they
gave her—" Andrew broke off as the front doorbell rang. He
went to answer it.

It was Simon Kemp. He arrived with a bucket of water,
drawn from his well, which he thought might be useful to
Andrew for washing purposes and to flush his lavatory,
though he warned him not to drink it without boiling it, as
he really did not know what condition the water was in.

He also explained, "I saw Peter arrive. He's come back
because of this thing about H.H., I suppose. I'd rather like to
talk to him, if that's possible."

"Come in," Andrew said. "He'll be glad to see you."

He took the bucket of water to the kitchen, indicating to
Kemp that he should go to the sitting-room. As he left the
two young men to meet, Andrew wondered if it was about
Ruth that he would find them talking when he joined them.
From what Kemp had said the day before in the Fidlers'
house, he thought that Peter must have been more involved
with her than he had felt it necessary to mention to Andrew.
However, when he went into the sitting-room he found that
it was the fate of Newsome's that they were discussing.

"I was over there yesterday," Kemp was saying. "There
weren't many of the chaps there because most of them are

still away on holiday, but the few of us who were there got gossiping as usual and there's a general idea about that Jack rather fancies himself as the future head. What d'you think about that?"

"If the school doesn't simply close down, you mean," Peter said.

"That's really going to happen, is it?" Kemp said. "I know there's been talk about it."

Peter looked at Andrew. "Tell Simon what you told me," he said.

Andrew told Kemp what Henry Hewison had told him about the financial troubles of the school. Kemp's square, snub-nosed face became extremely thoughtful as he listened.

"Of course I've seen warning signs for some time," he said. "I've been thinking of leaving, you know. I've found I don't much care for teaching and I've been wondering if I could get into farming somehow. I'd rather like to go abroad. But I've always felt a sort of loyalty to the place. H.H. was always very good to me and I felt he was trying to do a good job and one ought to support him, specially if he was having troubles. Then yesterday I heard the new head might be Jack, and I didn't feel the same about it any more. I can't exactly see him as head of Newsome's, can you?"

"That doesn't mean he can't see himself as that," Peter said. "In fact, it might be Jack who started the rumour."

"But you don't believe it?" Kemp said.

"My guess is, if the place survives, they'll bring in someone from outside," Peter answered. "There's always a lot to be said against internal appointments."

"Yes. Yes, of course." Kemp massaged the side of his jaw, his blue eyes gazing at some distant vision. "I wish I'd known this on Thursday."

"Why on Thursday?" Peter asked.

"Because Ruth and I had a long talk about these things

then. I believe if I promised we'd go off abroad, say to New Zealand, she might come back to me. But she doesn't believe I mean it when I talk about leaving here and now we can't discuss the subject at all without quarrelling. You still see her sometimes, don't you, Peter?"

"Now and then," Peter said.

"I expect you really understand her much better than I do. What's your honest opinion? Is there any chance she'd come back to me if I made a serious effort to get a job somewhere else?"

"I can't possibly make a guess at a thing like that," Peter answered. "You know what an unpredictable person she is. She's capable of doing things that nobody expects."

Kemp nodded his head sombrely. "The trouble is, I really love that damned girl, but that doesn't seem to help. No hurry about returning the bucket, Professor. I'll call in for it some time."

Peter went with him to the door and let him out.

When he returned he refilled his glass with beer, dropped onto the sofa and drew his feet up under him. Crouching there, wrapped up in his overcoat with its collar turned up, he looked very small and rather gnome-like, as if he had strayed into the room just to keep warm from some secret hiding-place in the garden.

"What's this about you and Ruth Hewison?" Andrew asked.

"Hockley," Peter said.

"Sorry, Hockley."

"Nothing."

"There was nothing between you?"

"Nothing at all."

"Then why does the poor chap think there was? At the Fidlers' he said he thought she'd married him on the rebound after an affair with you, and just now he said you probably understand her much better than he does."

"I probably do, but that doesn't mean we were ever in love with one another." Peter sipped some beer. "You know, Pickwick got it wrong. This is better than nothing, but what one wants at this time of day is something really hot. No, I think there's a simple explanation of why Ruth left him. She wanted to get away from her mother. It didn't occur to her when she got married that Simon had this thing about not letting H.H. down and was stubborn enough not to do what she wanted and that she was tying herself down to living within a stone's throw of Pauline. It's hard on Pauline. I believe she genuinely cares about the girl."

"What's Ruth got against her?" Andrew asked. "Would she always be interfering?"

"Well, you may think it's a bit of an obsession of mine," Peter said, "but I think Ruth's always believed her mother killed her husband. And though I don't think there was any special tie between Ruth and her stepfather, it may be a bit much to stomach a mother who's a murderess."

"So we get back to the Fidlers and did they lie to protect her? And why are they so concerned about her now and would they lie again if it would help her?" Andrew spread some more marmalade on the stale bread and, like Peter, yearned for coffee. "Do you think Fidler might have murdered Hewison to be made headmaster of the school? It doesn't matter whether or not there was any realistic probability of its happening, it would be enough if he thought there was. Can you imagine him doing such a thing, because, you see, he drove Hewison here from the school and if he lingered outside for a little after he'd dropped him off, he'd have seen there was no one at home here and that it was Mrs. Nesbit who let him in."

Peter shook his head. "No," he said.

"He wouldn't have done it?"

"Not for that reason."

"Even if he thought Pauline would put money into the

school if Hewison was out of the way, and out of gratitude for what he and Amabel had done for her when her husband was killed made it a condition of her giving the money that Fidler should be headmaster?"

Peter's face stayed blank for a moment, then a frown appeared on it.

"You're beginning to get me worried," he said.

"You think it sounds plausible?"

"Not really. I can't see anyone doing a murder for a reason like that. But all the same . . ."

"Well?"

"You're making me feel uncomfortable, as if you're getting somewhere near the truth. What about taking a walk in the village? It would warm us up and get our minds off all these things. Aren't there any odds and ends you want to buy at the shop?"

"Candles," Andrew said. "And I've run out of whisky. All right. But it's a bit early to go still. The shop may not be open. I'll have a wash in some of the water your friend brought us, and get dressed, and then we might think of going out."

He carried the breakfast tray out to the kitchen, took Simon Kemp's bucket upstairs, had an uncomfortable shave in cold water, washed, dressed and went downstairs again to find Peter sound asleep on the sofa.

Andrew realized that it must have been a very early plane that Peter had caught from Paris, that he had probably had very little sleep the night before and that now he was very tired. He had said that he would drive into Maddingleigh to obtain a new cylinder of gas, but Andrew felt reluctant to wake him.

Leaving him asleep, he only fetched a blanket from upstairs and spread it over Peter, who slept peacefully on until after eleven o'clock, when he woke abruptly and exclaimed with amazement at his having been asleep for so long when he had not meant to go to sleep at all. Andrew suggested that they might go out now to buy candles and food of some kind that they could eat in the evening and find out if it was possible to have lunch at the Green Dragon. The people there, of course, would be suffering from the power cut and the lack of water as much as the row of cottages here, but at least Andrew would be able to buy a bottle of whisky to bring home and it might be that the pub would be able to provide a meal of some sort.

It was twelve o'clock when he and Peter arrived there. As they left the cottage they had seen a man in a bright orange jerkin digging snow out of the ditches alongside the road. It seemed an aimless sort of occupation and Peter gave it as his opinion that the man was a detective, keeping an eye on them. In the shop they had joined with some other customers in their indignation at the inefficiency of the electricity board, then went on to the Green Dragon and in the bar found Mrs. Nesbit drinking gin and tonic in the company of a tall man whom she introduced to Andrew as her husband.

Mr. Nesbit was very tall, with a small head set high on a long, thin neck and a brightly coloured knitted cap hiding his hair, if in fact he had any. None of it showed. He had a sober, almost severe face which would have been quite without expression if it had not been that his eyes were singularly bright and shrewd. But as they moved from Andrew's face to Peter's, no other muscle moved in his. It appeared that he and Peter knew each other quite well. Each asked the other how he was and how things were going with him, each said that things weren't so bad considering, and as Peter ordered whisky for himself and Andrew and ascertained that they could be served with Cornish pasties, it appeared that the Nesbits had ordered Cornish pasties too and were only waiting at the bar for these to be delivered. As after a few minutes they were handed out, miraculously hot, they went to sit down at a table, and there, when their order had been handed over the bar, Andrew and Peter joined them.

Andrew realized that Peter had his reason for wanting to join the Nesbits and there were questions that he himself would have liked to ask Mr. Nesbit, but he left it to Peter to begin.

He plunged in almost immediately. "Mike, you've been doing a job for Mr. Hewison recently, I believe, making some bookshelves or something, haven't you?"

"That's right." Nesbit spoke with a lazy drawl with a strong Berkshire accent. "Job's nearly finished now, but naturally I haven't been up to the school since Thursday. I don't know whether I'm to finish the job or not. I'm waiting to be told."

"Yes, of course," Peter said. "Terrible thing, the way it happened."

"That's right," Nesbit repeated. "But people die in all kinds of peculiar ways. Really peculiar. I knew a case once when a woman died from licking paint."

"Licking paint?" Peter said incredulously.

"That's right."

"D'you mean she started sucking her paint brushes or something?"

"No, just licking the paint on her doorposts and suchlike. She was pregnant, see?" Nesbit's voice was as expressionless as his face. "You know how pregnant women get peculiar cravings. Well, hers was for licking paint. She was at it all the time when there was no one there to stop her. After she died they found the places where she'd licked the paint right off. They were on the doorposts and window-frames all round the house."

"But why should that have killed her?" Peter asked.

"Lead in the paint," Nesbit answered laconically. "Not allowed these days except for agricultural implements, but her husband used that kind of paint when he was redecorating the house. To save money, see? Killed her."

"You aren't suggesting he did it on purpose, are you?" Peter said. "How would he know she'd get a craving for licking paint? It isn't a thing many people get, so far as I know."

"As you say," Nesbit said. "But suppose he did know. Suppose she'd got the craving already when he painted the house. I've sometimes wondered. Make an interesting kind of murder case, wouldn't it? But I reckon the chances are he didn't know. Like how was I to know when I told Mr. Hewison . . . ?" He stopped and suddenly gave all his attention to his Cornish pasty.

"You told him something, did you?" Peter said.

"Now, Mike," his wife said, "you know we decided it didn't mean anything and had nothing to do with what happened to poor Mr. Hewison."

"That's right," her husband said.

"But what was it?" Peter pursued.

"Only about the box I found up at Godlingham House," Nesbit answered.

"What box?" Peter asked.

"A kind of box that might have held a revolver or something of the sort. I mean, there was kind of padding inside it and you could see the outline of the revolver where it had lain. And as nobody seemed to want it, I took it home and took out the padding and used it for keeping screws in. A nice sort of box, solid oak, well made. And I had it up at the school when I was working on Mr. Hewison's new bookshelves and I showed it to him and told him how I'd got it and said I hoped it wasn't something I oughtn't to have taken."

"But when did you take it?"

"When I was doing a job for the other Mr. Hewison. He wanted some shelves built into a room instead of the old cupboards as was there and he said all the junk inside the cupboards was to be thrown away. And there was this nice box. I've wondered sometimes if he just forgot about it and didn't mean it to be thrown away, but I took it home, and like I said, I've been keeping screws in it."

"But when were you doing this job at Godlingham House?"

"I reckon it'd be about six years ago. Matter of fact, it was the day he died. I'd been working there for several days. I remember that because it was when I first met my wife and we started going out together."

Peter leant his elbows on the table and took his chin in his hands. He had abandoned his pasty.

"Now let me get this straight," he said. "Just before the elder Mr. Hewison was killed you found a box in the house that looked as if it had once contained a revolver."

"That's right," Nesbit said.

"And you knew, did you, that Mr. Hewison had been shot but that no trace was ever found of the gun?"

Nesbit nodded.

"And it never occurred to you it might have come out of the box you found?"

"Why should it?" Nesbit asked. "It wasn't there when I found it. And it looked an old box. Nice, but old. The gun could have been missing out of it for years."

"People can be shot with very old weapons."

"But no one ever said anything about Mr. Hewison having a gun. If he'd had one he'd have had to have a licence for it, wouldn't he? And if he had a licence, the police would have found out about it."

"He ought to have had a licence, certainly. But if he'd had the gun for a long time, perhaps bought it abroad, he might not have bothered about a licence when he came home. He was in the Foreign Service and may have lived in places where it was normal to keep a gun in your house."

Mrs. Nesbit spoke up fiercely. "If Mike thought there was something wrong about taking the box, he wouldn't have told Mr. Hewison—I mean, Mr. Henry Hewison—about how he got it, would he? He was told all the things that came out of the old cupboards was going to be thrown away. There was nothing wrong about his taking it."

"Of course not," Peter said. "I'm only puzzled why he never said anything to the police about it. Didn't you know, Mike, they were hunting for a gun?"

A look of stubbornness faintly rearranged Nesbit's stern features.

"There wasn't any gun in it when I found it," he reiterated. "And I didn't want to get involved with the police. Who does? They never leave you in peace once you do. And it was none of my business."

Andrew entered the discussion. "Yet you're afraid that telling Mr. Hewison about the box and how you found it may have had something to do with his death. He told me on Thursday morning that he'd come by some curious information which he wanted to discuss with me, but he was killed before he could do that."

Nesbit's bright eyes swivelled from Peter's face to Andrew's.

"I'm not afraid," he said. "I'll tell them anything they want to know about the box if they ask me, but they haven't asked me anything yet."

"You could go to them with that information," Peter suggested.

Nesbit shook his head. "I don't want to get involved with them when likely as not it doesn't mean anything."

On their walk back from the Green Dragon to the cottage Andrew and Peter discussed whether or not it meant anything. If it did, Peter said, it was that the gun that had killed Charles Hewison had probably been his own, or at least it meant that at some time in his life he had possessed one. But

Peter was also of the opinion that even if the police might have been interested to hear about the box six years ago, they would not pay much attention to the story now. The padding inside it removed, scratched by the years when it had been used for storing screws, the box would not tell them anything that they could use in the investigation of the old murder and nothing at all about what had happened on Thursday evening. Nesbit's description of the box, as it had been when he found it, could hardly be accepted as evidence.

"All the same," Andrew said, "Henry Hewison thought it was evidence."

They had turned into the main road and were walking towards Peter's gate.

"You think that's what he wanted to discuss with you?" Peter said.

"Don't you?"

"I suppose so. And that chicken casserole you told me about which Mrs. Nesbit had left in the oven on the day of Charles Hewison's murder—you don't think that's important?"

"Not in itself."

"What do you mean by that?"

Andrew was not sure what he meant. Perhaps the casserole fitted into the puzzle somewhere, but he could not see how.

"It's just that I've been told Henry Hewison was sure Pauline had killed his brother and was always hunting for evidence to prove it," he said. "And if he suddenly heard that Charles and Pauline had had a gun in their house, which she could have used to kill her husband even if it totally vanished afterwards, he might have thought it was something worth discussing with someone whose approach would be what he called dispassionate."

They had passed the man in the orange jerkin, who was

still digging snow out of a ditch, had reached Peter's gate and started up the path to the house.

"He wasn't *sure* the thing was important," Andrew added. "If he had been he'd have gone straight to the police instead of trying it out on me first."

"Yes, I see." Peter opened the front door and the two of them kicked off their shoes, caked with snow, before advancing into the cottage. "How did the idea get around that we've a temperate climate?" he asked. "We get caught napping like this year after year, yet we do nothing effective about it. You know, you oughtn't to have let me sleep so long this morning. It's no good my going into Maddingleigh now to get a new gas cylinder for the radiator. They'll be shut on a Saturday afternoon."

"And if the Fidlers came for it, as they said they would," Andrew said, "it must have been while we were out. But the power cut really can't last much longer. I'm sure it'll come on again any time now."

Peter laughed. "I lack your confidence."

"Well, another thing I'm sure about," Andrew said as he padded into the sitting-room in his socks, wondering where he had left his slippers, "is that some more whisky would be very warming. I don't know about you, but I'm going to have another drink."

"That's a good idea," Peter agreed. "The best way to spend the time until the power comes on again will be to get really drunk. It'll stop us thinking about the cold, and about what we're going to eat this evening, and about the murder. Let's get started."

He took the basket of shopping that he was carrying out to the kitchen and returned after a minute or two with the bottle of whisky that they had bought that morning, glasses and a bottle of soda.

Presently, sitting with his back to the window with a glass of whisky, which had very little soda in it, in his hand, Andrew reflected that what he would really like at the moment was a glass of the finest Scotch malt whisky. It would penetrate his whole frame and bear him away to where moth and rust do not corrupt . . .

He pulled himself up. He had got involved with the wrong quotation. Moth and rust did not come into this story, nor did thieves break in and steal. Only murderers came from somewhere and broke into this nice little house and left a dreadful sense of corruption behind them. He began to mutter something else half-aloud.

"What was that?" Peter asked.

"Nothing," Andrew answered. "I was just saying something to myself about which I'm absolutely sure. I find it consoling after the last day or two to remember there are things I'm sure about. I happened to be thinking about malt whisky and I realized I was quite sure that, in malting, amylase will be released from the aleurone layer and will convert the starch in the endosperm to maltose. Now you can't cast doubts on that, can you?"

Peter gave him a sidelong look as if he were wondering if Andrew was becoming a little drunk already. But he did not think that he was. He was only exhausted by cold, discomfort, age, worry and a strange kind of fear and was trying somehow to escape into a world which he understood better.

"I didn't think scientific facts were as absolute as all that," Peter said. "Don't you have to keep modifying them?"

"Yes, but scientific generalizations provide a basis for unequivocal prediction," Andrew said. "Now in this case we've got ourselves involved in, I don't feel capable of predicting anything. I don't like it, Peter. I don't feel at home in it."

"And I'm afraid I'll never feel at home in your sort of science," Peter said. "I'll have to stick to my own kind, which I invent as I go along. Luckily for me, it's profitable and I find it fun. However, just at the moment I can predict something quite unequivocally. We're about to have a visitor."

He was standing at the window, looking out at the gleaming snow and the dignified façade of Godlingham House, but as he spoke he put down his glass and went to the door. As he did so, the bell rang.

Andrew heard him open the front door, then a woman's voice cry, "Peter! Simon told me you were here. Peter, you've got to help me!"

"Well, come along in," Peter said. "Come in and have a drink with Andrew and me and tell us all about it."

"I don't want a drink. There isn't time. I want you to come with me."

Andrew had recognized Ruth's voice. She seemed to be resisting Peter's effort to bring her inside, but then she gave in abruptly and came hurrying into the room. She looked pale and frightened. There were tears on her cheeks.

"It's all so awful," she said, on the edge of sobbing. "Peter, you've got to help me!"

She threw her arms round his neck. It was unlucky that she was so much taller than he was, for if what she wanted then was the support of a strong man onto whose breast she could throw herself, she had chosen someone of the wrong proportions. Andrew, old as he was, would have fulfilled her need better than Peter.

"Of course I'll help if I can," Peter said, muffled in her arms, "but what's the trouble?"

"They've found the gun," she said. "They found it in Simon's well. And they say the bullet that killed Henry came out of the same gun that killed my stepfather. They don't know if it was the gun they found today because they haven't had time to check it, but of course they think it is. It hasn't been long in the well, they do know that."

"But why on earth should Simon kill H.H. or your stepfather?" Peter asked.

"He didn't, he didn't, of course he didn't!"

"But they've arrested him?"

"They've taken him in for questioning. He's assisting them with their inquiries. Isn't that almost the same thing?"

"Not always. But what do you want me to do?"

"Come to the police station with me and explain to them about his alibi. Tell them we were in Croxley when Henry was killed. I could do it, but I feel so scared, I'll make a mess of it, and an alibi from a wife, even a separated one, isn't much good, is it? And you can make sure he gets a lawyer, if he needs one, because the poor darling won't know how to go about that himself. He's so good really, but he isn't very clever and he won't know how to protect himself and I don't either. I only know we ought to be doing something."

"All right, I'll come," Peter said, "though I don't expect I'll be able to help much. But of course I'll do what I can."

"Just a minute, Miss Hockley," Andrew said as she and Peter were turning towards the door. "May I ask you, just why are you so certain Mr. Kemp didn't murder Mr. Hewison? Is it only because of your knowledge of his character, or have you something concrete that Peter can use to help him?"

"I've something concrete," she said, "but I can't use it. That's what makes it so terrible."

"What is it?" Andrew asked.

"Only that I know my mother did it," she said. "And I know it because she told me so herself. Now let's go."

CHAPTER 8

For some time after they had gone Andrew stayed in the sitting-room, at first standing at the window, gazing out at the house across the road and thinking about the woman who lived in it, then sitting down with his back to the window and trying to think clearly about what he ought to do. He thought he knew what it was, but he shrank from taking upon himself what would in fact be great responsibilities. There had been a time when he had been used to taking all kinds of responsibility, but the last three years since his retirement had undermined his powers of resolution. No one nowadays expected him to interfere in their lives and he had developed a deep dislike of doing so.

But could he simply stay here and do nothing? That would have been an easier question to answer if he had been sure of a few more things than he was. But of one thing he was as sure as he was of anything to do with the process of malting and that was that Pauline Hewison had not murdered her brother-in-law.

Because his thoughts were drifting in an unconnected fashion, the old song by which his mind had been almost persecuted during the last few days started up in it once more. He caught himself humming it.

"There was a minnow went out for to winnow
On Christmas Day, on Christmas Day,
There was a minnow went out for to winnow
On Christmas Day in the morning.
There was a trout and he went out . . ."

Out! Of course that was the word that mattered. He went
out . . . Why had he not seen that before? Because of the
snow, that was just what the man would have done. Gone
out. And then come in again, bringing someone with
him . . .

At that moment the lights in the room came on.

They were unnecessary. It was not yet even dusk. They
only added a faintly sickly luminescence to the daylight.
After two days of pining for light, feeling almost that life
itself was grinding to a halt because of the lack of it, its
sudden reappearance was a disappointing anticlimax. But
almost at once a faint creaking sound in the radiators an-
nounced the fact that the electric pump had begun working
and was propelling water through them. How long it would
take for them to heat up and to warm the whole cottage
Andrew did not know, but to hurry the process, at least in
the sitting-room, he could switch on the electric fire, which
had stood useless in a corner since the power cut began.
When he had done that and seen its two bars grow wonder-
fully radiant and felt the sweet, benign warmth that came
from them, he turned off the unneeded lights, then went out
to the kitchen to see if there was any water in the main tap.

He turned it on and for a moment there was only a disappointing trickle, then suddenly water gushed forth. Grab-
bing the kettle, he filled it, plugged it in, reached for his
coffee-beans, poured them into Peter's electric grinder and
listened with an emotion approaching ecstasy to its whirring
as it reduced them to powder. Their aroma was exquisite
and life was back to normal. Life was splendid.

Then he switched off the kettle, abandoned the coffee-beans, put on his anorak and shoes and set off for the house across the road. For however splendid life might be, there were still duties to be performed from which it was important not to be seduced even by the scent of freshly ground coffee. He walked down to the road, crossed it, went in at the gates of Godlingham House and up the drive to the door.

Pauline Hewison's old red Mini was standing in front of it and the door was open. She was in the doorway, apparently just about to come out and pull the door shut behind her. Seeing Andrew, she stood still.

"It's you," she said. "It's a funny thing, but I've had a feeling you and I might have something more to say to each other sooner or later."

"May I come in?" he asked. "Or am I stopping you going out?"

"It's nothing that can't wait." She gave a strange little laugh. "Come in."

She thrust the door open and led him into her high, beautiful drawing-room.

A log fire was alight in the grate, as it had been on Thursday evening, but it had almost smouldered away to ashes, as if no one had paid it any attention for some time, but the great crystal chandelier, hanging from the centre of the ceiling, was ablaze. She did not trouble to turn it off, though its light was not needed, and she did not stir up the fire, but threw herself down in a chair by the fireplace, looking at Andrew with her dark, intent stare, and said challengingly, "Well?"

Her face was very pale without her heavy make-up and showed lines which made her look older than he had ever seen her look before.

He took a chair facing her on the other side of the fireplace.

"Why did you tell your daughter you killed Henry Hewison?" he asked.

"Because I did," she said, "so it seemed the simplest thing to do."

He shook his head. "You didn't."

"It's going to be very easy for the police to prove I did," she said.

"And very easy for me to prove you did not," he answered.

He looked at her thoughtfully. She was in her duffle-coat and trousers, with the coat hanging open, showing the white sweater under it, the only clothes in which he had ever seen her, and he caught himself wondering how she would look in something long and shimmering, with jewels in her ears and at her throat. Very handsome, he thought, very desirable. Not that that was the sort of thing to be thinking about now.

"You don't want me to prove you didn't, do you?" he said.

"That depends."

"On who else is going to be suspected? It won't be Kemp. I shouldn't be surprised if they've let him go by now. They've nothing against him except that they found the gun in his well and anyone could have thrown it there."

"Myself included."

"No, I don't think that would have been possible."

"How do you make that out?"

"I'll tell you in a moment. Tell me first why you told Ruth you killed Henry Hewison."

"It seemed to be the best thing I could do for her. She was frantic when the police came for Simon. She's very much in love with him, you know. She'd never have left him if it hadn't meant living so close to me. And he's a stubborn dolt and couldn't see that."

"Does she hate you so much?"

"I think so."

"Yet she said she couldn't use what you'd told her about having committed the murder, even to help Kemp."

"Did she?" She looked sceptical.

"Yes, and she was crying about it."

"Well, no one likes to have a mother who's a murderess." There was mockery in her voice. "She was probably crying for herself as much as for me. I haven't been a very successful mother. First I brought her into the world before I'd any right to—I'm sure you realize that, I was only fifteen when she was born—and her father was only seventeen and disappeared in a hurry when he knew she was on the way. And later, when I tried to supply her with another father, it happened that the job of the man I married kept taking him around the world at different times, so that she spent most of her childhood in boarding-schools. Excellent, very expensive ones, because Charles was a very rich man and he was generous enough, but still, it wasn't home and when he and she met they were always quite indifferent to one another. And since the police are going to get around to arresting me sooner or later, why shouldn't I try to do something to help her straight away? Let her know her Simon's safe without her having to go through hours, or even days, of agony."

"Tell me then, when did you throw the gun into the well?"

"When?" For an instant she looked disconcerted, then she shrugged her shoulders. "On Thursday night, of course."

"With the police swarming all over the place till I don't know when in the morning and keeping an eye on us all ever since. They haven't been particularly obtrusive, but there's a man out there, wasting time clearing snow out of the ditches, who I'm sure has watched all your comings and goings and those of the rest of us too. No, I think there's only one time when the gun could have been thrown into the well and that was immediately after the murder, before the police got here, and I happen to be able to say you didn't do it then because I was with you. But that isn't the only thing that's against you as a murderess."

She lifted her eyebrows in ironic curiosity.

"Yes," Andrew went on, "whoever killed Henry Hewison knew he'd be in that house alone. I realize he could have let you know earlier in the day that he was coming to see me. I don't see why he should have done that, but it's possible. But it wasn't possible for you to know that my train would be late and that he'd stay there in the darkness for quite a long time, waiting for me. So unless you came over cold-bloodedly prepared to do a double murder, you don't seem to me a very good suspect. It's true you might have been down in the road just by chance when he arrived in Fidler's car and when Mrs. Nesbit, who'd just got off the bus from Maddingleigh, went up the path to the house with him and let him in. If that had happened and you'd stayed there to watch, you'd have realized there was no one in there with him. But I imagine you wouldn't have had a gun in your pocket. I shouldn't think it was a thing you carried around with you as a general rule in case you should feel a call to use it. So you'd have had to come back to this house to get it and then go over to the cottage to do the shooting. But it happens you were seen going up to the cottage at least a little while before I appeared on the scene."

"Who saw me arrive?" she asked quickly.

"Hannah Goodchild."

"That woman! You needn't believe anything she says about me."

"But what she says happens to clear you, even though she didn't intend that it should, because somehow I feel that if you'd shot Hewison you wouldn't have lingered about afterwards till I arrived, but would have got away as fast as you could, particularly as he didn't die on the spot. If you'd stayed at all, when you realized he was alive, it would have been to put a second shot into him, and that wouldn't have taken you long. You'd have been gone for sure before I got there."

"Then what had I been doing in the cottage from the time I was seen till you arrived?"

"What I think happened," Andrew said, "is that you went over, just as you told me, because that evening you couldn't stand being alone. The snow and the power cut brought back too vividly the night when your husband was killed. And Ruth had gone out to see Simon and the Portuguese couple who work for you had gone home for Christmas, so the place may have been full of ghosts and for once you needed the company of someone to help you dispel them. And I was a stranger. You weren't on good terms with any of your other neighbours. You could hardly turn to them for help. But there was nothing to stop you calling on me and inviting me to sit by your fire and eat some hot food. So you went over and you found the door open. I suppose you rang the bell and nobody answered. So perhaps you called out—of course I don't know exactly what happened—but I should imagine you'd call out and you'd still get no answer and you were a little worried by that open door, so you risked going in to make sure things were all right, and as soon as you got to the door of the sitting-room, you stumbled over Hewison's body."

She gave a smile that tightened her features into a nervous grimace. "D'you know, you sound much more as if you're accusing me of a murder than clearing me of one? You sound very fierce."

"Do I?" Andrew said. "I'm sorry, I didn't mean to."

"But I'm interested. Go on. What did I do next?"

"I think in the darkness you took for granted it was me and that I'd probably had a heart attack or something like that and your first thought then would have been that you'd got to get to the telephone to call a doctor. In the process, I suppose, you found the torch which Hewison had dropped when he was shot, and when you did that you discovered who it was who'd been killed. Not that he was dead yet. For all I know he spoke to you. Perhaps he even told you who'd shot him. Did he?"

"What do you think?"

"I think he probably did and because of what he told you, you didn't telephone the doctor, but sat down and considered what you ought to do."

"So you *are* accusing me of murder. Wasn't it murder to sit there and think while he was dying?"

"A few minutes weren't going to make any difference to him. He was a dead man already. No doctor, even if he'd miraculously got there in a few minutes, could have saved him."

"So I left him, did I, and went out and was just going to close the door when you arrived?"

"That's what I think you did. And you'd absent-mindedly taken his torch with you and that proves a good deal of what I'm saying. I know he had a torch when he arrived at the cottage, because Mrs. Nesbit remembers seeing him use it when he was looking for the doorbell, yet the police didn't find one in the cottage. And Mrs. Goodchild says you weren't using one when she saw you go up to the door. So you must have been inside the cottage before I arrived to have been able to pick it up."

Pauline gave a deep sigh and her slim body relaxed in her chair, as if she found a relief in abandoning her struggle against him.

"You're right in almost every detail," she said, "except one."

"Which is that?" Andrew asked.

"He didn't tell me who shot him. He didn't speak at all, except for that one word he said to you before he died."

"But you knew who'd done it, or why did you linger instead of phoning at once for a doctor?"

"Why should knowing it have stopped me doing that?"

"Because you were afraid to tell what you knew."

"Why was I afraid? D'you mean you think I believed it was Ruth and that I wanted to protect her?"

"I don't think you thought for a moment it was Ruth, even though you took the guilt of the murder on yourself today at least partly to set her mind at rest about her husband. And though I don't know you very well, I think it's possible you feel at least partly guilty because of the way you sat there thinking, and you're tired of guilt. You've lived with it far too long and it's left you weary and empty. Because you did kill your husband, didn't you, Mrs. Hewison?"

She did not answer. Turning slightly in her chair, she fixed her gaze on the dying fire. As dusk deepened outside, the light in the room from the chandelier seemed to grow brighter and lit up her drawn features harshly.

"D'you know what I was doing before you arrived here?" she said in a low voice.

"Seeing you by your car and knowing you'd confessed to a murder," Andrew answered, "I couldn't help wondering if you were preparing a get-away."

She leant her cheek on her hand and went on murmuring to the fire. "A get-away, yes, that's just what I'd been doing. And suppose I'd insisted on going instead of bringing you in here, would you have let me go?"

"I could hardly have stopped you. You look a strong woman and I'm a little past the age for a rough-and-tumble."

"And you wouldn't really have wanted to stop me. You don't like what you're doing now. You only came to see me and talk like this to make sure you were right about who murdered Henry."

"It was Fidler, of course."

"Of course. But do you know why he did it?"

"Oddly enough, I think it was to protect you."

"I suppose you could put it like that."

"It might be more accurate to say it was to protect his source of income. You've been his source of income ever since he gave you an alibi for the murder of your husband, haven't you? And I think a part of your motive for confessing to a murder you hadn't committed was to take revenge on him for the long years of blackmail. He and his wife got desperate, you know, when they discovered you were under suspicion. They wanted to protect you at all costs, because if you were arrested that comfortable income you've been paying them was going to stop. It's ironic that the murder Fidler committed to stop your guilt of that earlier murder being revealed by Hewison should backfire as it did and leave you the chief suspect. But of course he couldn't know you were going to have that sudden impulse to seek my company. When they realized how strong the case against you was and that Mrs. Goodchild was going to do all she could to make it stick, Amabel even tried to make out a case against Peter, that he'd murdered Hewison in mistake for me."

"Amabel—ah yes, she's the strong-minded one, the greedy one. If it hadn't been for her I think I could have paid Jack off and gone away. It was she who wanted to keep me where they were sure I was in their power and couldn't quietly vanish away and stop the payments."

"Fidler told me Hewison had a hold on you and that that was why you stayed. I suppose that was just to put me off the scent. But didn't you realize they were as much in your power as you were in theirs? Being accessory after the fact and blackmail itself are both very serious offences. If they'd given you away to the police about that alibi, you could have given them away."

"Yes, it was all that that I was thinking about as I sat in your cottage, watching Henry die. I wondered if I dared let Jack be accused of the murder. Because if that had happened

he'd have told everything and I didn't know whether or not
I'd the courage to face that. But at the beginning, after
Charles's death, I was in a state of shock at what I'd done and
simply did what the Fidlers told me. And by the time I'd
come out of that and begun to think for myself, I'd simply
stopped caring what happened to me. I thought of suicide. I
even took a bottleful of pills one night, but next day I found I
was still alive and I hadn't the courage to repeat it. I've
never done anything right all my life. I made a bad beginning and I kept it up." She stirred, suddenly sitting upright
in her chair and staring at him. "Why am I talking to you like
this?"

"I suppose you've wanted to talk to someone for a long
time," Andrew said. "Ruth guessed a good deal of it. She told
me the first time we met that she thought your heart was
broken."

"She's wrong. I haven't got a heart to break."

"I believe if you really hadn't you wouldn't be aware of
the fact. But I can understand you couldn't talk to a daughter. It would be putting a too terrible burden on her."

"Oh no, I couldn't have talked to Ruth." She made a gesture with one hand, brushing that possibility aside. "But how
do you know all this? How do you know what I did to Charles
and about the blackmail?"

"It was the blackmail I guessed at first," Andrew said. "It
began with my guessing Goodchild had been a doctor. I
thought of that when I saw him lift Hewison's eyelid and
shine his torch right into his eye and then say definitely that
he was dead. It was only a man with medical training, I
thought, who'd have done that. And I mentioned that to the
Fidlers and they told me then that they'd guessed it themselves when he handled Amabel's wrist when she thought
she'd broken it and he told her she hadn't. But then Fidler
made a mistake. He told me how he'd looked into old
records and found out that Goodchild had been struck off

the register for getting a girl of fifteen pregnant and that the girl's name was Pauline Hockley. Amabel tried to stop him telling me the story, but she couldn't do it, he enjoyed it too much. And so I began to wonder what kind of man it was who'd have gone to the trouble of raking up that kind of dirt after so many years, and the only answer I could think of was someone who thought he might make something out of it. A blackmailer. I don't know if he ever tried blackmailing Goodchild. I doubt it rather, because the amount he could have paid wouldn't have been worth the trouble, and I think Hannah Goodchild would have torn Fidler's eyes out if he'd tried to harry her husband. She might even have gone to the police about it. But it started me thinking about that alibi the Fidlers gave you and wondering how much you'd had to pay for it."

"Plenty," Pauline answered. "Plenty."

"Fidler saw you kill your husband, didn't he?"

"Yes, he came over to see why I hadn't come to tea with them. They thought it was because of the snow, that I might have slipped and fallen on the way over to them, or something like that, because when I didn't come they telephoned and I didn't answer. A kindly impulse of theirs really, which is funny, isn't it? And he was actually looking in at the window when I did it."

"Why didn't you answer the telephone?"

"To explain that I'd have to go right back to the beginning." She gave another deep sigh, relaxing again and turning her gaze back to the ashes in the grate, which were only a soft, flaky, grey mass with very few glowing sparks left in it.

Andrew said nothing, waiting to see whether or not she meant to go on. For a while it seemed almost as if she had forgotten that he was there. Then she said, "I haven't told you what I was doing before you came. I was writing a letter. It's there on the bureau. It's to that man, Ashe, that superintendent, and it tells him everything, except that I didn't

actually accuse Jack of Henry's murder. I said I knew he had
the gun, but I couldn't prove anything. I still don't see how
you can prove it."

Andrew glanced towards the bureau, on the open lid of
which he saw an envelope with a single name written on it,
but as far as he could see from that distance, no address.

"We know Fidler gave Hewison a lift from the school to
Peter's gate," he said. "And we know Hewison had been told
recently by Nesbit that he'd found a box that had once held a
gun here in your house, just before your husband's death,
when Nesbit came to put up some shelves for him. Hewison
told me he had some information he wanted to discuss with
me and I believe it was about that box. And I think he told
Fidler about it during that drive from the school and chal-
lenged him about the alibi he'd given you, not realizing how
dangerous it was to do that. For Fidler saw at once how
disastrous it could be for you and for his private income if
the possession of a gun could be traced to you. So he didn't
hesitate to act. I don't know where he'd kept the gun all
these years. Perhaps at first, while the police were still hunting for it, he kept it hidden up at the school, but later I
suppose he brought it back to his house and when he saw
Mrs. Nesbit let Hewison into the cottage and realized I
wasn't there, he went and got it, went back to the cottage,
rang the bell, was let in by Hewison, and Fidler made him
back along the passage to the sitting-room doorway and shot
him there. He didn't do it straight away at the front door
because the noise of the shot would have been more likely to
be heard there. Then he left, but didn't close the door properly. He must have been in a panic that I might appear at
any moment and he didn't take the trouble to make sure the
latch had caught, but simply bolted home. Then he must
have made his way from his own garden into Kemp's and
thrown the gun into the old well. His footsteps might have
been visible in the snow if it hadn't come on to snow again

soon after that, but in fact, you remember, it did and they'd soon have vanished."

She nodded absently. "Yes, it makes sense. But to go back to the beginning . . ." She again fell silent and again Andrew waited.

After a long pause, with her gaze still bent on the last remnant of the fire, she went on, "I suppose you could say my mother was at the bottom of it all. She's been dead for many years, so it doesn't matter what I say about her. She was a patient of Godfrey Goodchild's in Durham, where we lived, and unfortunately for him and for me, she fell in love with him. I remember he was very handsome in those days and he was a shy, gentle sort of man, as he still is, and she thought she could do what she liked with him. She was a strong, violent woman. There's very little affection in my memory of her, though I suppose I'm rather like her. But it turned out she couldn't get anywhere with Godfrey. He'd recently married Hannah and no one else existed for him. And that was more than my mother could bear, so when she discovered I was pregnant she accused Godfrey of being the father. It was sheer spite, nothing else. At first I denied it. Ruth's father, I told you, was a boy in the Army, and the Army was the only thing he cared about, and we both knew that if it turned out he'd been sleeping with a girl of my age he'd be in serious trouble. So I promised him I'd never say anything about him and he went away and I never saw him again. Then my mother started putting pressure on me to accuse Godfrey and because I was frightened of her and didn't really understand what I was doing, I said all the things she wanted and they were believed, and that, of course, ruined him. Don't think I'm trying to excuse myself. Young as I was, I could have fought her. But I didn't. It may surprise you, but I believe I regret what I did to Godfrey more than having shot my husband."

"Which I suppose had something to do with finding that

the Goodchilds were living here when you bought this house," Andrew said.

"Yes, it all goes back to that," she answered. "The sheer chance that we came to live here when we might have gone anywhere else in the country—anywhere in the whole world, because, as I said, Charles was very rich. And when Godfrey and I first met he didn't even recognize me and I thought I might manage to keep quiet about who I was, and if I had, none of these awful things need have happened. But Ruth told Hannah one day that her name was Hockley and Hannah remembered it at once and I had a terrible scene with her. You may not think I look as if I'm easily frightened, but I am. She frightened me just as my mother used to when she got into a rage, so I promised her I'd go away and Godfrey need never know anything about it. But of course I couldn't simply vanish without explaining the situation to Charles and Ruth and when I did . . ." She gave a sudden shudder and again fell silent.

"When you did, your husband refused to move," Godfrey prompted her.

She nodded without speaking.

"Did he know the Goodchild story?" he asked.

"He knew that Ruth was illegitimate and that I'd only been fifteen when she was born," she said, "but he didn't know I'd accused the wrong man of being her father, or what that had done to him. I met Charles when he was on leave in London and I was a secretary in a solicitor's office, the solicitor who was handling his inheritance. I wasn't in love with him—I've never been in love with anyone since that boy I knew when I was a child—but it wasn't entirely for the money either. It was for the safety, the security Charles could give me. He could send Ruth to school and look after her and I didn't have to go on worrying about what would happen to her if I lost my job or got ill. Of course, becoming one of the idle rich was very pleasant, but it wasn't for that I married him."

"Or killed him? You didn't shoot him because he was going to make over a lot of money to Newsome's?'"

"It never even entered my head. No, I killed him because he refused to move away from Godlingham. Isn't that funny, when I've lived on here ever since? It was on an afternoon like this, except that it was still snowing heavily, that I told him the story about Godfrey and how I'd promised I'd go away. We were in the room we called the study and Charles was cleaning his gun. He'd bought it when he was in Aden and things were dangerous. He'd never used it once, but he treasured it and looked after it and when he wanted something to do he'd get it out and oil it. And there it was in his hand while I was standing before him, telling him what I'd done to Godfrey and that we'd got to leave the place because I couldn't face living across the road from the man I'd wronged. And Charles told me not to be ridiculous. He said I'd better learn to live with what I'd done and he wouldn't dream of moving. So we began to quarrel violently, as we did rather often, and he told me that if I wouldn't drop this whole idea and be quiet he'd telephone Henry straight away and tell him he could have as much money as he liked for Newsome's, and I told him to go ahead and do it."

"And he did?"

"Yes."

"And you shot him immediately afterwards?"

"Almost immediately. You see, while he was doing it he put the gun down on the table and I suddenly got the idea that I'd sooner kill myself than go on living the false sort of life I was used to, with too much on my conscience, and I suddenly grabbed the gun and held it to my head. It was loaded. He always kept it loaded, as he used to in Aden. And he slammed down the telephone and lunged for the gun and I struggled to keep it, and then—it went off."

"So it wasn't murder, it was an accident."

"I wish I could say that. I've been trying to say it to myself at intervals for the last six years. But it isn't true. For just an instant I wanted to kill him. I was in a state of blind rage and terror by then, and it only takes an instant to pull a trigger. And in only an instant he was lying at my feet, dead."

"And that's when Fidler came on the scene."

She gave another of her painful smiles. "Do you know, you sound far less hard on me now that I'm confessing to a murder I really committed than you did when I was trying to confess to one I hadn't? You're a curious sort of man. What are you going to do with me?"

"I don't see how I can do anything. If you want to take that letter you've written to Superintendent Ashe in Maddingleigh, I can't see why I should stop you."

She turned her head suddenly, gave him a long, steady look, then laughed abruptly.

"And I look a strong woman and you're a bit old for a rough-and-tumble, isn't that what you said? So when I want to go, I can go."

He did not answer.

After a moment she went on, "Yes, Jack was looking in at the window and saw it happen. When he'd telephoned, Charles and I had been in the middle of our quarrel, shouting things at each other, and we hadn't troubled to answer. I believe Mrs. Nesbit telephoned too, but we didn't answer her either. So because it surprised Jack and Amabel that the house seemed to be empty, he came over to see if things were all right and he arrived just as I pulled the trigger. And I've been in his power ever since."

Andrew nodded. "Yes, he went *out* . . . And I suppose he took charge at that point."

"Yes, he took the gun away from me," Pauline said. "I remember he was wearing gloves. He pointed that out to me later and said my fingerprints would be on the gun, but his wouldn't, although he'd handled it. I don't know if that was true. I've been told a gun doesn't take fingerprints. Anyway, that doesn't matter. He grabbed me by the arm and hurried me off to their house and on the way he smashed the kitchen window from outside and said that would make it look as if someone had broken in. Later I said some money was missing, though it wasn't really. And when we got into the Fidlers' house the telephone was ringing and Amabel had just gone to answer it, but when she'd said only a few words he took it away from her and answered it. It was Mrs. Nesbit who was ringing up to tell me she couldn't get back from Maddingleigh and that she'd left a chicken casserole for me in the oven. I forgot all about it and it worried her. I think it almost made her suspicious of me. But even if I'd remembered it, I shouldn't have been able to eat anything that night."

"She told me you made yourself a meal of bacon and eggs and coffee."

"Oh, that." She gave her odd laugh again. "Bob Grace, the constable in the village, spent the whole night in the house, so I had to give him something. But how did you know about that?"

"It was just that our power cut on Thursday reminded her of it and she told me the whole story. I think I began to be a little suspicious of Fidler then. It didn't surprise me in the circumstances that you'd forgotten the casserole, but there was something queer about the way he'd snatched the telephone away from his wife, when she was a more suitable person to take a message from Mrs. Nesbit than he was."

"Yes, I see. And is that all?"

"All?"

"Yes, have we any more to say to one another?"

"D'you know, I don't believe we have. I think we've covered most of the ground."

"Then, if you don't mind, I'll leave you." She came to her

feet in a swift, graceful movement. "You're the best listener I've ever known. I'm grateful. My mind's more at rest than it's been for a long time. Goodbye, Professor Basnett."

"Goodbye, Mrs. Hewison."

She went out quickly and he made no movement to stop her.

It was not until he had heard the sound of the Mini starting up outside and was sure that she had driven away that he stood up and crossed to the bureau where the letter to Superintendent Ashe was lying. For a moment he thought that he ought to take it to the police station in Maddingleigh, but then he left it where it was and returned to Peter's cottage.

"Of course, you knew she meant to kill herself," Superintendent Ashe said next morning when he called in on Peter and Andrew to tell them what had happened the evening before.

Andrew shook his head. "I couldn't possibly guess what was going on in the mind of a woman like her."

One of the things that Ashe had told them was that when Pauline Hewison had driven out of the gates of Godlingham House the man in the orange jerkin, who had still been very slowly and incompetently clearing the ditches of snow, had leapt into a car which had been inconspicuously parked behind a clump of trees and had followed her. She had driven straight to Newsome's. There she had knocked on the side door, which opened on to the staircase that led up to Henry Hewison's flat, had brushed aside the lame old caretaker when he came to answer it, thrusting her way past him into the main school building, and then had raced up the stairs that led to the tower which jutted up at one end of the old house. It contained the water tanks that supplied the school and it was the highest building anywhere in the neighbourhood. Perhaps she had known that she was being followed, for she had not hesitated when she reached the top, but had opened a window there and thrown herself out. When the detective reached her spread-eagled body, she was dead.

When Andrew had heard this from the superintendent he had told him most of what had passed between Pauline and himself in their long interview and made sure that the letter addressed to Ashe had reached him. It had, handed over to him by Ruth, who had found it when she and Simon Kemp had returned to the house not long after Andrew had left it. It seemed to Andrew that almost everything that Pauline had told him had been in the letter, but Ashe had gone through it, step by step, wanting Andrew's confirmation of what she had said. Already, Ashe told him, Jack and Amabel Fidler had been taken to Maddingleigh for questioning, and the probability was, he said, that Fidler would be charged with murder, along with one or two relatively minor crimes, such as being accessory after the fact and extortion.

Ashe drank two cups of the deliciously hot coffee, which it had been possible for Andrew to make for breakfast, now that the power had been restored, made one more unsuccessful attempt to persuade him to admit that he had known Pauline had intended to commit suicide when she left him, then left himself.

Peter helped himself to more coffee and said, "But you did know she was going to kill herself, didn't you?"

The cottage was delightfully warm and the sunlight on the snow outside filled the room with brightness, making it seem a splendidly safe refuge from the cruelty, though happily not the sparkling beauty of winter.

"If I admitted it, would you think I was wicked?"

"Is that how you feel yourself?"

"Well, almost from the time I arrived here I've felt there was wickedness in the atmosphere, and at the moment I'm wondering how much of it was in myself. Yes, I guessed. She'd told me she'd already made two attempts to kill herself, so it seemed fairly likely she'd try again. People with a tendency that way do that, I believe. But I've been saying to myself, at least she did what she wanted, and I hope, if ever I want the same thing for myself, say because I've got some incurable illness I can't face, that no one tries to stop me. She'd an incurable illness, of course, one she couldn't live with any longer."

"An illness?" Peter said. "I didn't know that."

"Yes, the sense of guilt."

"I see. But it's an irony, isn't it, that the murder she didn't commit finished her, not the one she confessed to? Also that Charles's money will keep Newsome's going, at least for a time, when poor old H.H. isn't there to enjoy it. Her right to the money will be cancelled, since she's confessed she killed Charles and so it will go to his next of kin, and I'm sure H.H. left everything he had to the school. And Ruth will get nothing. That's rather hard on her, but perhaps it will be a good thing in the end. She and Simon will start again from scratch. I understood yesterday she's going back to him and he's going to do his best to find a farming job in New Zealand. You know, she always suspected her mother of killing Charles. That's why she couldn't face living here."

Andrew nodded. "Knowing that was another of the burdens Pauline couldn't carry, because I believe, after her fashion, she was fond of Ruth. As fond, at least, as she ever was of anyone after her soldier left her. Peter, will it put you out very much if I don't stay on here, but go back to London? I can't see myself settling down now to work quietly for the rest of the winter after what's happened."

"That's all right," Peter said. "I didn't expect you to stay. I'll lock the place up and go back to Paris. Mrs. Nesbit will look after it while I'm away, and I may feel more like facing it myself again in the spring."

"The decorators must be nearly finished in my flat by now," Andrew said.

He felt a great longing for his flat, for its privacy, for the feeling he had that it was home, for the kindly ghost of Nell that it would always harbour. He was curious to see too how he would like the new colours that he had chosen and thought that even if the decorators had not quite finished and still played their radio at all hours, loudly exchanged opinions from room to room about football and wanted cups of tea, he would not, after all, find it too difficult to endure.